Lolly Willowes
or the Loving Huntsman

LOLLY WILLOWES

or the Loving Huntsman

Sylvia Townsend Warner

GENERAL PRESS

Published by
GENERAL PRESS
4805/24, Fourth Floor, Krishna House
Ansari Road, Daryaganj, New Delhi - 110002
Ph : 011-23282971, 45795759
E-mail : generalpressindia@gmail.com

www.generalpress.in

First Edition : 2023

ISBN : 9789354995156

Published by Azeem Ahmad Khan for General Press

Contents

PART I

When her father died, Laura Willowes went to live in London with her elder brother and his family.

'Of course,' said Caroline, 'you will come to us.'

'But it will upset all your plans. It will give you so much trouble. Are you sure you really want me?'

'Oh dear, yes.'

Caroline spoke affectionately, but her thoughts were elsewhere. They had already journeyed back to London to buy an eiderdown for the bed in the small spare-room. If the wash-stand were moved towards the door, would it be possible to fit in a writing-table between it and the fireplace? Perhaps a bureau would be better, because of the extra drawers? Yes, that was it. Lolly could bring the little walnut bureau with the false handles on one side and the top that jumped up when you touched the spring by the ink-well. It had belonged to Lolly's mother, and Lolly had always used it, so Sibyl could not raise any objections. Sibyl had no claim to it whatever, really. She had only been married to James for two years, and if the bureau had marked the morning-room wall-paper, she could easily put something else in its place. A stand with ferns and potted plants would look very nice.

Lolly was a gentle creature, and the little girls loved her; she would soon fit into her new home. The small spare-room would be rather a loss. They could not give up the large spareroom to Lolly, and the small spare-room was the handiest of the two for ordinary visitors. It seemed extravagant to wash a pair of the large linen sheets for a single guest who came but for a couple of nights. Still, there it was, and Henry was right – Lolly ought to come to them. London would be a pleasant change for her. She would meet nice people, and in London she would have a better chance of marrying. Lolly was twenty-eight. She would have to make haste if she were going to find a husband before she was thirty. Poor Lolly! black was not becoming to her. She looked sallow, and her pale grey eyes were paler and more surprising than ever underneath that very unbecoming black mushroom hat. Mourning was never satisfactory if one bought it in a country town.

While these thoughts passed through Caroline's mind, Laura was not thinking at all. She had picked a red geranium flower, and was staining her left wrist with the juice of its crushed petals. So, when she was younger, she had stained her pale cheeks, and had bent over the greenhouse tank to see what she looked like. But the greenhouse tank showed only a dark shadowy Laura, very dark and smooth like the lady in the old holy painting that hung in the dining-room and was called the Leonardo.

'The girls will be delighted,' said Caroline. Laura roused herself. It was all settled, then, and she was going to live in London with Henry, and Caroline his wife, and Fancy and Marion his daughters. She would become an inmate of the tall house in Apsley Terrace where hitherto she had only been a country sister-in-law on a visit. She would recognise a special something in the physiognomy of that housefront which would enable her to stop certainly before it without glancing at the number or the door-knocker. Within it, she would know unhesitatingly which of the polished brown doors was which, and become quite indifferent to the position of the cistern, which had baffled her so one night when she lay awake trying to assemble the house inside the box of its outer walls. She would take the air in Hyde Park and watch the children on their ponies and the fashionable trim ladies in Rotten Row, and go to the theatre in a cab.

London life was very full and exciting. There were the shops, processions of the Royal Family and of the unemployed, the gold tunnel at Whiteley's, and the brilliance of the streets by night. She thought of the street lamps, so impartial, so imperturbable in their stately diminuendos, and felt herself abashed before their scrutiny. Each in turn would hand her on, her and her shadow, as she walked the unfathomed streets and squares – but they would be familiar then – complying with the sealed orders of the future; and presently she would be taking them for granted, as the Londoners do. But in London there would be no greenhouse with a glossy tank, and no apple-room, and no potting-shed, earthy and warm, with bunches of poppy heads hanging from the ceiling, and sunflower seeds in a wooden box, and bulbs in thick paper bags, and hanks of tarred string, and lavender drying on a tea-tray. She must leave all this behind, or only enjoy it as a visitor, unless James and Sibyl happened to feel, as Henry and Caroline did, that of course she must live with them.

Sibyl said: 'Dearest Lolly! So Henry and Caroline are to have you.... We shall miss you more than I can say, but of course you will prefer London. Dear old London with its picturesque fogs and its interesting people, and all. I quite envy you. But you mustn't quite forsake Lady Place. You must come and pay us long visits, so that Tito doesn't forget his aunt.'

'Will you miss me, Tito?' said Laura, and stooped down to lay her face against his prickly bib and his smooth, warm head. Tito fastened his hands round her finger.

'I'm sure he'll miss your ring, Lolly,' said Sibyl. 'You'll have to cut the rest of your teeth on the poor old coral when Auntie Lolly goes, won't you, my angel?'

'I'll give him the ring if you think he'll really miss it, Sibyl.'

Sibyl's eyes glowed; but she said:

'Oh no, Lolly, I couldn't think of taking it. Why, it's a family ring.'

When Fancy Willowes had grown up, and married, and lost her husband in the war, and driven a lorry for the Government, and married again from patriotic motives, she said to Owen Wolf-Saunders, her second husband:

'How unenterprising women were in the old days! Look at Aunt Lolly. Grandfathei left her five hundred a year, and she was nearly thirty when he died, and yet she could find nothing better to do than to settle down with Mum and Dad, and stay there ever since.'

'The position of single women was very different twenty years ago,' answered Mr. Wolf-Saunders. 'Feme soul, you know, and feme covert, and all that sort of rot.'

Even in 1902 there were some forward spirits who wondered why that Miss Willowes, who was quite well off, and not likely to marry, did not make a home for herself and take up something artistic or emancipated. Such possibilities did not occur to any of Laura's relations. Her father being dead, they took it for granted that she should be absorbed into the household of one brother or the other. And Laura, feeling rather as if she were a piece of family property forgotten in the will, was ready to be disposed of as they should think best.

The point of view was old-fashioned, but the Willoweses were a conservative family and kept to old-fashioned ways. Preference, not prejudice, made them faithful to their past. They slept in beds and sat upon chairs whose comfort insensibly persuaded them into respect for the good sense of their forbears. Finding that well-chosen wood and well-chosen wine improved with keeping, they believed that the same law applied to well-chosen ways. Moderation, civil speaking, leisure of the mind and a handsome simplicity were canons of behaviour imposed upon them by the example of their ancestors.

Observing those canons, no member of the Willowes family had risen too much eminence. Perhaps great-great-aunt Salome had made the nearest approach to fame. It was a decent family boast that great-great-aunt Salome's puff-paste had been commended by King George in. And great-great-aunt Salome's prayer-book, with the services for King Charles the Martyr and the Restoration of the Royal Family and the welfare of the House of Hanover – a nice example of impartial piety – was always used by the wife of the head of the family. Salome, though married to a Canon of Salisbury, had taken off her embroidered kid gloves, turned up her sleeves, and gone into the kitchen to mix the paste for His Majesty's eating, her Ven icepoint lappets dangling above the floury bowl. She was a loyal subject, a devout church woman, and a good housewife, and the Willoweses were properly proud of her. Titus, her father, had made a voyage to the Indies, and had brought back with him a green parrokeet, the first of its kind to be seen in Dorset. The parrokeet was named Ratafee, and lived for fifteen years. When he died he was stuffed; and perched as in life upon his ring, he swung from the cornice of the china-cupboard surveying four generations of the Willowes family with his glass eyes. Early in the nineteenth century one eye fell out and was lost. The eye which replaced it was larger, but inferior both in lustre and expressiveness. This gave Ratafee a rather leering look, but it did not compromise the esteem in which he was held. In a humble way the bird had made county history, and the family acknowledged it, and gave him a niche in their own.

Beside the china-cupboard and beneath Ratafee stood Emma's harp, a green harp ornamented with gilt scrolls and acanthus leaves in the David manner. When Laura was little she would sometimes steal into the empty drawing-room and pluck the strings which remained unbroken. They answered with a melancholy and distracted voice, and Laura would pleasantly frighten herself with the thought of Emma's ghost coming back to make music with cold fingers, stealing into the empty drawing-room as noiselessly as she had done. But Emma's was a gentle ghost. Emma had died of a decline, and when she lay dead with a bunch of snowdrops under her folded palms a lock of her hair was cut off to be embroidered into a picture of a willow tree exhaling its branches above a padded white satin tomb. 'That,' said Laura's mother, 'is an heirloom of your great-aunt Emma who died.' And Laura was sorry for the poor young lady who alone, it seemed to her, of all her relations had had the misfortune to die.

Henry, born in 1818, grandfather to Laura and nephew to Emma, became head of the house of Willowes when he was but twenty-four, his father and unmarried elder brother dying of smallpox within a fortnight of each other. As a young man Henry had shown a roving and untraditional temperament, so it was fortunate that he had the licence of a cadet to go his own way. He had taken advantage of this freedom to marry a Welsh lady, and to settle near Yeovil, where his father bought him a partnership in a brewery. It was natural to expect that upon becoming the head of the family Henry would abandon, if not the Welsh wife and the brewery, at least Somerset, and return to his native place. But this he would not do. He had become attached to the neighbourhood where he had spent the first years of his married life; the ill-considered jest of his uncle the Admiral, that Henry was courting a Welshwoman with a tall hat like Mother Shipton's who would carry her shoes to church, had secretly estranged him from his relations; and – most weighty reason of all – Lady Place, a small solid mansion, which he had long coveted – saying to himself that if ever he were rich enough he would make his wife the mistress of it – just then came into the market. The Willowes obstinacy, which had for so long kept unchanged the home in Dorset, was now to transfer that home across the county border. The old house was sold, and the furniture and family belongings were installed at Lady Place. Several strings of Emma's harp were broken, some feathers were jolted out of Ratafee's tail, and Mrs. Willowes, whose upbringing had been Evangelical, was distressed for several Sundays by the goings-on that she found in Salome's prayer-book. But in the main the Willowes tradition stood the move very well. The tables and chairs and cabinets stood in the same relation to each other as before; the pictures hung in the same order though on new walls; and the Dorset hills were still to be seen from the windows, though now from windows facing south instead of from windows facing north. Even the brewery, untraditional as it was, soon weathered and became indistinguishably part of the Willowes way of life.

Henry Willowes had three sons and four daughters. Everard, the eldest son, married his second cousin, Miss Frances D'Urfey. She brought some more Willowes property to the Somerset house: a set of garnets; a buff and gold tea-service bequeathed her by the Admiral, an amateur of china, who had dowered all his nieces and great-nieces with Worcester, Minton, and Oriental; and two oil-paintings by Italian masters which the younger Titus, Emma's brother, had bought in Rome whilst travelling for his health. She bore Everard three children: Henry, born in 1867; James, born in 1869; and Laura, born in 1874.

On Henry's birth Everard laid down twelve dozen of port against his coming of age. Everard was proud of the brewery, and declared that beer was the befitting drink for all classes of Englishmen, to be preferred over foreign wines. But he did not extend this ban to port and sherry; it was clarets he particularly despised.

Another twelve dozen of port was laid down for James, and there it seemed likely the matter would end.

Everard was a lover of womankind; he greatly desired a daughter, and when he got one she was all the dearer for coming when he had almost given up hope of her. His delight upon this occasion, however, could not be so compactly expressed. He could not lay down port for Laura. At last he hit upon the solution of his difficulty. Going up to London upon the mysterious and inadequate pretext of growing bald, he returned with a little string of pearls, small and evenly matched, which exactly fitted the baby's neck. Year by year, he explained, the necklace could be extended until it encircled the neck of a grown-up young woman at her first ball. The ball, he went on to say, must take place in winter, for he wished to see Laura trimmed with ermine. 'My dear,' said Mrs. Willowes, 'the poor girl will look like a Beefeater.' But Everard was not to be put off. A stuffed ermine which he had known as a boy was still his ideal of the enchanted princess, so pure and sleek was it, and so artfully poised the small neat head on the long throat. 'Weasel!' exclaimed his wife. 'Everard, how dare you love a minx?'Laura escaped the usual lot of the new-born, for she was not at all red. To Everard she seemed his very ermine come to true life. He was in love with her femininity from the moment he set eyes on her. 'Oh, the fine little lady!' he cried out when she was first shown to him, wrapped in shawls, and whimpering at the keen sunlight of a frosty December morning. Three days after that it thawed, and Mr. Willowes rode to hounds. But he came back after the first kill. ''Twas a vixen,' he said. 'Such a pretty young vixen. It put me in mind of my own, and I thought I'd ride back to see how she was behaving. Here's the brush.'

Laura grew up almost as an only child. By the time she was past her babyhood her brothers had gone to school. When they came back for their holidays, Mrs. Willowes would say: 'Now, play nicely with Laura. She has fed your rabbits every day while you have been at school. But don't let her fall into the pond.'

Henry and James did their best to observe their mother's bidding. When Laura went too near the edge of the pond one or the other would generally remember to call her back again; and before they returned to the house, Henry, as a measure of precaution, would pull a wisp of grass and wipe off any tell-tale green slime that happened to be on her slippers. But nice play with a sister so much younger than themselves was scarcely possible. They performed the brotherly office of teaching her to throw and to catch; and when they played at Knights or Red Indians, Laura was dutifully cast for some passive female part. This satisfied the claims of honour; if at some later stage it was discovered that the captive princess or the faithful squaw had slipped away unnoticed to the company of Brewer in the coachhouse or Oliver Cromwell the toad, who lived under the low russet roof of violet leaves near the disused melon pit, it did not much affect the course of the drama. Once, indeed, when Laura as a captive princess had been tied to a tree, her brothers were so much carried away by a series of single combats for her favour that they forgot to come and rescue her before they swore friendship and went off to the Holy Land. Mr. Willowes, coming home from the brewery through a sunset haze of midges, chanced to stroll into the orchard to see if the rabbits had barked any more of his saplings. There he found Laura, sitting contentedly in hayband fetters, and singing herself a story about a snake that had no mackintosh. Mr. Willowes was extremely vexed when he understood from Laura's nonchalant account what had happened. He took off her slippers and chafed her feet. Then he carried her indoors to his study, giving orders that a tumbler of hot sweet lemonade should be prepared for her immediately. She drank it sitting on his knee while he told her about the new ferret. When Henry and James were heard approaching with war-whoops, Mr. Willowes put her into his leather arm-chair and went out to meet them. Their warwhoops quavered and ceased as they caught sight of their father's stern face. Dusk seemed to fall on them with condemnation as he reminded them that it was past their supper-time, and pointed out that, had he not happened upon her, Laura would still have been sitting bound to the Bon Chrétien pear-tree.

This befell upon one of the days when Mrs. Willowes was lying down with a headache. 'Something always goes wrong when I have one of my days,' the poor lady would complain. It was also upon one of Mrs. Willowes's days that Everard fed Laura with the preserved cherries out of the drawing-room cake. Laura soon became very sick, and the stable-boy was sent off post-haste upon Everard's mare to summon the doctor.

Mrs. Willowes made a poor recovery after Laura's birth; as time went on, she became more and more invalidish, though always pleasantly so. She was seldom well enough to entertain, so Laura grew up in a quiet household. Ladies in mantles of silk or of sealskin, according to the season of the year, would come to call, and sitting by the sofa would say: 'Laura is growing a big girl now. I suppose before long you will be sending her to a school.' Mrs. Willowes heard them with half-shut eyes. Holding her head deprecatingly upon one side, she returned evasive answers. When by quite shutting her eyes she had persuaded them to go, she would call Laura and say: 'Darling, aren't your skirts getting a little short?'

Then Nannie would let out another tuck in Laura's ginghams and merinos, and some months would pass before the ladies returned to the attack. They all liked Mrs. Willowes, but they were agreed amongst themselves that she needed bracing up to a sense of her responsibilities, especially her responsibilities about Laura. It really was not right that Laura should be left so much to herself. Poor dear Miss Taylor was an excellent creature. Had she not inquired about peninsulas in all the neighbouring schoolrooms of consequence? But Miss Taylor for three hours daily and Mme. Brevet's dancing classes in winter did not, could not, supply all Laura's needs. She should have the companionship of girls of her own age, or she might grow up eccentric. Another little hint to Mrs. Willowes would surely open the poor lady's eyes. But though Mrs. Willowes received their good counsel with a flattering air of being just about to become impressed by it, and filled up their tea-cups with a great deal of delicious cream, the silk and sealskin ladies hinted in vain, for Laura was still at home when her mother died.

During the last few years of her life Mrs. Willowes grew continually more skilled in evading responsibilities, and her death seemed but the final perfected expression of this skill. It was as if she had said, yawning a delicate cat's yawn, 'I think I will go to my grave now,' and had left the room, her white shawl trailing behind her.

Laura mourned for her mother in skirts that almost reached the ground, for Miss Boddie, the family dressmaker, had nice sensibilities and did not think that legs could look sorrowful. Indeed, Laura's legs were very slim and frisky, they liked climbing trees and jumping over haycocks, they had no wish to retire from the world and belong to a young lady. But when she had put on the new clothes that smelt so queerly, and looking in the mirror saw herself sad and grown-up, Laura accepted the inevitable. Sooner or later she must be subdued into young-ladyhood; and it seemed befitting that the change should come gravely, rather than with the conventional polite uproar and fuss of 'coming-out' – which odd term meant, as far as she could see, and when once the champagne bottles were emptied and the flimsy ball-dress lifted off the thin shoulders, going-in.

As things were, she had a recompense for the loss of her liberty. For Everard needed comfort, he needed a woman to comfort him, and abetted by Miss Boddie's insinuations Laura was soon able to persuade him that her comfortings were of the legitimate womanly kind. It was easy, much easier than she had supposed, to be grown-up; to be clear-headed and watchful, to move sedately and think before she spoke. Already her hands looked much whiter on the black lap. She could not take her mother's place – that was as impossible as to have her mother's touch on the piano, for Mrs. Willowes had learnt from a former pupil of Field, she had the jeu perlé; but she could take a place of her own. So Laura behaved very well – said the Willowes connection, agreeing and approving amongst themselves – and went about her business, and only cried when alone in the potting-shed, where a pair of old gardening gloves repeated to her the shape of her mother's hands.

Her behaviour was the more important ir? that neither of her brothers was at home when Mrs. Willowes died. Henry, now a member of the Inner Temple, had just proposed marriage to a Miss Caroline Fawcett. When he returned to London after the funeral it was impossible not to feel that he was travelling out of the shadow that rested upon Lady Place to bask in his private glory of a suitable engagement.

He left his father and sister to find consolation in consoling each other. For though James was with them, and though his sorrow was without qualification, they were not likely to get much help from James. He had been in Germany studying chemistry, and when they sent off the telegram Everard and Laura reckoned up how long he would take to reach Lady Place, and planned how they could most comfortingly receive him, for they had already begun to weave a thicker clothing of family kindness against the chill of bereavement. On hearing the crunch of the wagonette in the drive, and the swishing of the wet rhododendrons, they glanced at each other reassuringly, taking heart at the thought of the bright fire in his bedroom, the carefully chosen supper that awaited him. But when he stood before them and they looked at his red twitching face, they were abashed before the austerity of a grief so differently sustained from their own. Nothing they had to offer could remedy that heart-ache. They left him to himself, and sought refuge in each other's society, as much from his sorrow as theirs, and in his company they sat quietly, like two good children in the presence of a more grown-up grief than they could understand.

James might have accepted their self-effacement with silent gratitude; or he might not have noticed it at all – it was impossible to tell. Soon after his return he did a thing so unprecedented in the annals of the family that it could only be explained by the extreme exaltation of mind which possessed him: for without consulting any one, he altered the furniture, transferring a mirror and an almond-green brocade settee from his mother's room to his own. This accomplished, he came slowly downstairs and went out into the stable-yard where Laura and his father were looking at a litter of puppies. He told them what he had done, speaking drily, as of some everyday occurrence, and when they, a little timidly, tried to answer as if they too thought it a very natural and convenient arrangement, he added that he did not intend to go back to Germany, but would stay henceforth at Lady Place and help his father with the brewery.

Everard was much pleased at this. His faith in the merits of brewing had been rudely jolted by the refusal of his eldest son to have anything to do with it. Even before Henry left school his ambition was set on the law. Hearing him speak in the School Debating Society, one of the masters told him that he had a legal mind. This compliment left him with no doubts as to what career he wished to follow, and before long the legal mind was brought to bear upon his parents. Everard was hurt, and Mrs. Willowes was slightly contemptuous, for she had the old-fashioned prejudice against the learned professions, and thought her son did ill in not choosing to live by his industry rather than by his wits. But Henry had as much of the Willowes determination as either his father or his mother, and his stock of it was twenty-five years younger and livelier than theirs. 'Times are changed,' said Everard. 'A country business doesn't look the same to a young man as it did in my day.'

So though a partnership in the brewery seemed the natural destiny for James, Everard was much flattered by his decision, and hastened to put into practice the scientific improvements which his son suggested. Though by nature mistrustful of innovations he hoped that James might be innocently distracted from his grief by these interests, and gave him a new hopper in the same paternal spirit as formerly he had given him a rook-rifle. James was quite satisfied with the working of the hopper. But it was not possible to discover if it had assuaged his grief, because he concealed his feelings too closely, becoming, by a hyperbole of reticence, reserved even about his reserve, so that to all appearances he was no more than a red-faced young man with a moderate flow of conversation.

Everard and Laura never reached that stage of familiarity with James which allows members of the same family to accept each other on surface values. Their love for him was tinged with awe, the awe that love learns in the moment of finding itself unavailing. But they were glad to have him with them, especially Everard, who was growing old enough to like the prospect of easing his responsibilities, even the inherent responsibility of being a Willowes, on to younger shoulders. No one was better fitted to take up this burden than James. Everything about him, from his seat on a horse to his taste in leather bindings, betokened an integrity of good taste and good sense, unostentatious, haughty, and discriminating.

The leather bindings were soon in Laura's hands. New books were just what she wanted, for she had almost come to the end of the books in the Lady Place library. Had they known this the silk and sealskin ladies would have shaken their heads over her upbringing even more deploringly. But, naturally, it had not occurred to them that a young lady of their acquaintance should be under no restrictions as to what she read, and Mrs. Willowes had not seen any reason for making them better informed.

So Laura read undisturbed, and without disturbing anybody, for the conversation at local tea-parties and balls never happened to give her an opportunity of mentioning anything that she had learnt from Locke on the Understanding or Glanvil on Witches. In fact, as she was generally ignorant of the books which their daughters were allowed to read, the neighbouring mammas considered her rather ignorant. However they did not like her any the worse for this, for her ignorance, if not so sexually displeasing as learning, was of so unsweetened a quality as to be wholly without attraction. Nor had they any more reason to be dissatisfied with her appearance. What beauties of person she had were as unsweetened as her beauties of mind, and her air of fine breeding made her look older than her age.

Laura was of a middle height, thin, and rather pointed. Her skin was brown, inclining to sallowness; it seemed browner still by contrast with her eyes, which were large, set wide apart, and of that shade of grey which inclines neither to blue nor green, but seems only a much diluted black. Such eyes are rare in any face, and rarer still in conjunction with a brown colouring. In Laura's case the effect was too startling to be agreeable. Strangers thought her remarkable-looking, but got no further, and those more accustomed thought her plain. Only Everard and James might have called her pretty, had they been asked for an opinion. This would not have been only the partiality of one Willowes for another. They had seen her at home, where animation brought colour into her cheeks and spirit into her bearing. Abroad, and in company, she was not animated. She disliked going out, she seldom attended any but those formal parties at which the attendance of Miss Willowes of Lady Place was an obligatory civility; and she found there little reason for animation. Being without coquetry she did not feel herself bound to feign a degree of entertainment which she had not experienced, and the same deficiency made her insensible to the duty of every marriageable young woman to be charming, whether her charm be directed towards one special object or, in default of that, universally distributed through a disinterested love of humanity. This may have been due to her upbringing – such was the local explanation. But her upbringing had only furthered a temperamental indifference to the need of getting married – or, indeed, of doing anything positive – and this indifference was reinforced by the circumstances which had made her so closely her father's companion.

There is nothing more endangering to a young woman's normal inclination towards young men than an intimacy with a man twice her own age. Laura compared with her father all the young men whom otherwise she might have accepted without any comparisons whatever as suitable objects for her intentions, and she did not find them support the comparison at all well. They were energetic, good-looking, and shot pheasants with great skill; or they were witty, elegantly dressed, and had a London club; but still she had no mind to quit her father's company for theirs, even if they should show clear signs of desiring her to do so, and till then she paid them little attention in thought or deed.

When Aunt Emmy came back from India and filled the spare-room with cedar-wood boxes, she exclaimed briskly to Everard: 'My dear, it's high time Laura married! Why isn't she married already?' Then, seeing a slight spasm of distress at this barrack-square trenchancy pass over her brother's face, she added: 'A girl like Laura has only to make her choice. Those Welsh eyes… Whenever they look at me I am reminded of Mamma. Everard! You must let me give her a season in India.'

'You must ask Laura,' said Everard. And they went out into the orchard together, where Emmy picked up the windfall apples and ate them with the greed of the exile. Nothing more was said just then. Emmy was aware of her false step. Ashamed at having exceeded a Willowes decorum of intervention she welcomed this chance to reinstate herself in her brother's good graces by an evocation of their childhood under these same trees.

But Everard kept silence for distress. He believed in good faith that his relief at seeing Laura's budding suitors nipped in their bud was due to the conviction that not one of them was good enough for her. As innocently as the unconcerned Laura might have done, but did not, he waited for the ideal wooer.

Now Emmy's tactless concern had thrown a cold shadow over the remoter future after his death. And for the near future had she not spoken of taking Laura to India? He would be good. He would not say a word to dissuade the girl from what might prove to be to her advantage. But at the idea of her leaving him for a country so distant, for a manner of life so unfamiliar, the warmth went out of his days.

Emmy unfolded her plan to Laura; that is to say, unfolded the outer wrappings of it. Laura listened with delight to her aunt's tales of Indian life. Compounds and mangoes, the early morning rides along the Kilpawk Road, the grunting song of the porters who carried Mem Sahibs in litters up to the hill-stations, parrots flying through the jungle, ayahs with rubies in their nostrils, kid-gloves preserved in pickle jars with screw-tops – all the solemn and simple pomp of old-fashioned Madras beckoned to her, beckoned like the dark arms tinkling with bangles of soft gold and coloured glass. But when the beckonings took the form of Aunt Emmy's circumstantial invitation Laura held back, demurred this way and that, and pronounced at last the refusal which had been implicit in her mind from the moment the invitation was given.

She did not want to leave her father, nor did she want to leave Lady Place. Her life perfectly contented her. She had no wish for ways other than those she had grown up in. With an easy diligence she played her part as mistress of the house, abetted at every turn by country servants of long tenure, as enamoured of the comfortable amble of day by day as she was. At certain seasons a fresh resinous smell would haunt the house like some rustic spirit. It was Mrs. Bonnet making the traditional beeswax polish that alone could be trusted to give the proper lustre to the elegantly bulging fronts of taiboys and cabinets. The grey days of early February were tinged with tropical odours by great-great-aunt Salome's recipe for marmalade; and on the afternoon of Good Friday, if it were fine, the stuffed foxes and otters were taken out of their glass cases, brushed, and set to sweeten on the lawn.

These were old institutions, they dated from long before Laura's day. But the gradual deposit of family customs was always going on, and within her own memory the sum of Willowes ways had been augmented. There was the Midsummer Night's Eve picnic in Potts's Dingle – cold pigeon-pie and cider-cup, and moth-beset candles flickering on the grass. There was the ceremony of the hop-garland, which James had brought back from Germany, and the pantomime party from the workhouse, and a very special kind of sealing-wax that could only be procured from Padua. Long ago the children had been allowed to choose their birthday dinners, and still upon the seventeenth of July James ate duck and green peas and a gooseberry fool, while a cock-pheasant in all the glory of tail-feathers was set before Laura upon the ninth of December. And at the bottom of the orchard flourished unchecked a bed of nettles, for Nannie Quantrell placed much trust in the property of young nettles eaten as spring greens to clear the blood, quoting emphatically and rhythmically a rhyme her grandmother had taught her:

'If they would eat nettles in March
And drink mugwort in May,
So many fine young maidens
Would not go to the clay.'

Laura would very willingly have drunk mugwort in May also, for this rhyme of Nannie's, so often and so impressively rehearsed, had taken fast hold of her imagination. She had always had a taste for botany, she had also inherited a fancy for brewing. One of her earliest pleasures had been to go with Everard to the brewery and look into the great vats while he, holding her firmly with his left hand, with his right plunged a long stick through the clotted froth which, working and murmuring, gradually gave way until far below through the tumbling, dissolving rent the beer was disclosed.

Botany and brewery she now combined into one pursuit, for at the spur of Nannie's rhyme she turned her attention into the forsaken green byways of the rural pharmacopoeia. From Everard she got a little still, from the family recipe-books much information and good advice; and where these failed her, Nicholas Culpepper or old Goody Andrews, who might have been Nicholas's crony by the respect she had for the moon, were ready to help her out. She roved the countryside for herbs and simples, and many were the washes and decoctions that she made from sweet-gale, water purslane, cowslips, and the roots of succory, while her salads gathered in fields and hedges were eaten by Everard, at first in hope and trust, and afterwards with flattering appetite. Encouraged by him, she even wrote a little book called 'Health by the Wayside' commending the use of old-fashioned simples and healing herbs. It was published anonymously at the local press, and fell quite flat. Everard felt much more slighted by this than she did, and bought up the remainders without telling her so. But mugwort was not included in the book, for she was never allowed to test its virtues, and she would not include recipes which she had not tried herself. Nannie believed it to be no less effective than nettles, but she did not know how to prepare it. Once long ago she had made a broth by seething the leaves in boiling water, which she then strained off and gave to Henry and James. But it made them both sick, and Mrs. Willowes had forbidden its further use. Laura felt positive that mugwort tea would not have made her sick. She begged for leave to make trial of it, but to no avail; Nannie's prohibition was as absolute as that of her mistress. But Nannie had not lost her faith. She explained that the right mugwort for the purpose was a very special kind that did not grow in Somerset, but at the gates of the cobbler in her native village the mugwort grew fair enough. Long after this discussion had taken place, Laura found in Aubrey's Miscellany a passage quoted from Pliny which told how Artemis had revealed the virtues of mugwort to the dreaming Pericles. She hastened to tell Nannie of this. Nannie was gratified, but she would not admit that her faith needed any buttressing. 'Those Greeks didn't know everything!' she said, and drove a needle into her red cloth emery case, which was shaped like a strawberry and spotted over with small yellow beads.

For nearly ten years Laura kept house for Everard and James. Nothing happened to disturb the easy serenity of their days except the birth of first one daughter and then another to Henry and Caroline, and this did not disturb it much. Everard, so happy in a daughter, was prepared to be happy in granddaughters also. When Henry apologised to him with dignity for the accident of their sex Everard quoted to him the nursery rhyme about what little boys and girls were made of. Henry was relieved to find his father taking so lightly a possible failure in the Willowes inale line, but he wished the old man wouldn't trifle so. He could not stoop to give his father the lie over this unscientific theory of sex. He observed gloomily that daughters could be very expensive now that so much fuss was being made about the education of women.

Henry in his fears for the Willowes' male line had taken it for granted that his brother would never marry. And certainly if to lie very low about a thing is a sign that one is not thinking about it, James had no thought of marriage. He was nearly thirty-three when he announced with his usual quiet abruptness that he was going to marry. The lady of his choice was a Miss Sibyl Mauleverer. She was the daughter of a clergyman, but of a fashionable London clergyman which no doubt accounted for her not being in the least like any clergyman's daughter seen by Everard and Laura hitherto. Miss Mauleverer's skirts were so long and so lavish that they lay in folds upon the ground all round her when she stood still, and required to be lifted in both hands before she could walk. Her hats were further off her head than any hats that had yet been seen in Somerset, and she had one of the up-to-date smooth Aberdeen terriers. It was indeed hard to believe that this distinguished creature had been born and bred in a parish. But nothing could have been more parochial than her determination to love her new relations and to be loved in return. She called Everard Vaterlein, she taught Laura to dance the cake-walk, she taught Mrs. Bonnet to make petits canapés à l'Impératrice; having failed to teach Brewer how to make a rock garden, she talked of making one herself; and though she would have liked old oak better, she professed herself enchanted by the Willowes walnut and mahogany. So assiduously did this pretty young person seek to please that Laura and Everard would have been churlish had they not responded to her blandishments. Each, indeed, secretly wondered what James could see in any one so showy and dashing as Sibyl. But they were too discreet to admit this, even one to the other, and contented themselves with politely wondering what Sibyl could see in such a country sobersides as James.

Lady Place was a large house, and it seemed proper that James should bring his wife to live there. It also seemed proper that she should take Laura's place as mistress of the household. The sisters-in-law disputed this point with much civility, each insisting upon the other's claim like two queens curtseying in a doorway. However Sibyl was the visiting queen and had to yield to Laura in civility, and assume the responsibilities of housekeeping. She jingled them very lightly, and as soon as she found herself to be with child she gave them over again to Laura, who made a point of ordering the petits canapés whenever anyone came to dinner.

Whatever small doubts and regrets Everard and Laura had nursed about James's wife were put away when Sibyl bore a man child. It would not have been loyal to the heir of the Willowes to suppose that his mother was not quite as well-bred as he. Everard did not even need to remind himself of the Duchess of Suffolk. Titus, sprawling his fat hands over his mother's bosom, Titus, a disembodied cooing of contentment in the nursery overhead, would have justified a far more questionable match than James had made.

A year later Everard, amid solemnity, lit the solitary candle of his grandson's first birthday upon the cake that Mrs. Bonnet had made, that Laura had iced, that Sibyl had wreathed with flowers. The flame wavered a little in the draught, and Everard, careful against omens, ordered the French windows to be shut. On so glowing a September afternoon it was strange to see the conifers nodding their heads in the wind and to hear the harsh breath of autumn go forebodingly round the house. Laura gazed at the candle. She understood her father's alarm and, superstitious also, held her breath until she saw the flame straighten itself and the first little trickle of coloured wax flow down upon the glittering tin star that held the candle. That evening, after dinner, there was a show of fireworks for the school children in the garden. So many rockets were let off by Everard and James that for a while the northern sky was laced with a thicket of bright sedge scattering a fiery pollen. So hot and excited did Everard become in manoeuvring this splendour that he forgot the cold wind and took off his coat.

Two days after he complained of a pain in his side. The doctor looked grave as he came out of the bed-chamber, though within it Laura had heard him laughing with his old friend, and rallying him upon his nightcap. Everard had inflammation of the lungs, he told her; he would send for two nurses. They came, and their starched white aprons looked to her like unlettered tombstones. From the beginning her soul had crouched in apprehension, and indeed there was at no time much hope for the old man. When he was conscious he lay very peacefully, his face turned towards the window, watching the swallows fly restlessly from tree to tree. 'It will be a hard winter,' he said to Laura. 'They're gathering early to go.' And then: 'Do you suppose they know where they're going?'

'I'm sure they do,' she answered, thinking to comfort him. He regarded her shrewdly, smiled, and shook his head. 'Then they're wiser than we.'

When grandfather Henry, that masterful man, removed across the border, he was followed by a patriarchal train of manservants and maidservants, mares, geldings, and spaniels, vans full of household stuff, and slow country waggons loaded with nodding greenery. 'I want to make sure of a good eating apple,' said he, 'since I am going to Lady Place for life.' Death was another matter. The Willowes burial-ground was in Dorset, nor would Henry lie elsewhere. Now it was Everard's turn. The dead appeared to welcome him without astonishment – the former Everards and Ti tuses, Lauras and Emmelines; they were sure that he would come, they approved his decision to join them.

Laura stood by the open grave, but the heap of raw earth and the planks sprawling upon it displeased her. Her eyes strayed to the graves that were completed. Her mind told the tale of them, for she knew them well Four times a year Mrs. Willowes had visited the family burying place, and as a child Laura had counted it a solemn and delicious honour to accompany her upon these expeditions. In summer especially, it was pleasant to sit on the churchyard wall under the thick roof of lime trees, or to finger the headstones, now hot, now cold, while her mother went from grave to grave with her gauntlet gloves and her gardening basket. Afterwards they would eat their sandwiches in a hayfield, and pay a visit to old Mrs. Dymond, whose sons and grandsons in hereditary office clipped the grass and trimmed the bushes of the family enclosure. As Laura grew older the active part of these excursions fell upon her; and often of late years when she went alone she half yielded her mind to the fancy that the dead mother whose grave she tended was sitting a little apart in the shade, presently to rise and come to meet her, having just recalled and delicately elaborated some odd trait of a neighbouring great-uncle.

The bees droned in the motionless lime trees. A hot ginny churchyard smell detached itself in a leisurely way from the evergreens when the mourners brushed by them. The sun, but an hour or so declined, shone with an ardent and steadfast interest upon the little group. 'In the midst of life we are in death,' said Mr. Warbury, his voice sounding rather shameless taken out of church and displayed upon the basking echoless air. 'In the midst of death we are in life,' Laura thought, would be a more accurate expression of the moment. Her small body encased in tremendous sunlight seemed to throb with an intense vitality, impersonally responding to heat, scent, and colour. With blind clear-sighted eyes she saw the coffin lowered into the grave, and the earth shovelled in on top of it. She was aware of movement around her, of a loosening texture of onlookers, of footsteps and departures. But it did not occur to her that the time was come when she too must depart. She stood and watched the sexton, who had set to work now in a more business-like fashion. An arm was put through hers. A voice said: 'Dear Laura! we must go now,' and Caroline led her away. Tears ran down Caroline's face; she seemed to be weeping because it was time to go.

Laura would have turned for one more backward look, but Caroline prevented her. Her tears ran faster and she shook her head and sighed. They reached the gate. It closed behind them with a contented click, for they were the last to leave.

Opposite the churchyard were the gates of the old home. The drive was long, straight, and formal; it had been a cart-track across a meadow when the old home was a farm. At the end of the drive stood the grey stone house. A purple clematis muffled the porch, and a white cat lay asleep in a bed of nasturtiums. The blinds were drawn down in respect to the dead. Laura looked at it. Since her earliest childhood it had been a familiar sight, a familiar thought. But now she saw it with different eyes: a prescience of exile came over her and, forgetting Lady Place, she looked with the yearning of an outcast at the dwelling so long ago discarded. The house was like an old blind nurse sitting in the sun and ruminating past events. It seemed an act of the most horrible ingratitude to leave it all and go away without one word of love. But the gates were shut, the time of welcome was gone by.

For a while they stood in the road, none making a move, each waiting for the other's lead. A tall poplar grew on the left hand of the churchyard gate. Its scant shadow scarcely indented the white surface of the road. A quantity of wasps were buzzing about its trunk, and presently one of the wasps stung Henry. This seemed to be the spur that they were all waiting for; they turned and walked to the corner of the road where the carriages stood that were to drive them back to the station.

Everyone was sorry for Laura, for they knew how much she had loved her father. They agreed that it was a good thing that Henry and Caroline were taking her to London. They hoped that this change would distract her from her grief. Meanwhile, there was a good deal to do, and that also was a distraction. Clothes and belongings had to be sorted out, friends and family pensioners visited, and letters of condolence answered. Beside this she had her own personal accumulation of vagrant odds and ends to dispose of. She had lived for twenty-eight years in a house where there was no lack of cupboard room, and a tradition of hoarding, so the accumulation was considerable. There were old toys, letters, stones of strange shapes or bright colours, lesson-books, water-colour sketches of the dogs and the garden; a bunch of dance programmes kept for the sake of their little pencils, and all the little pencils tangled into an inextricable knot; pieces of unfinished needlework, jeweller's boxes, scraps cut out of the newspaper, and unexplainable objects that could only be remembrancers of things she had forgotten. To go over these hoards amused the surface of her mind. But with everything thrown away she seemed to be denying the significance of her youth.

Thus busied, she was withheld all day from her proper care. But at dusk she would go out of the house and pace up and down the nut alley at the foot of the garden. The cold airs that rose up from the ground spoke sadly to her of burial, the mossy paths were hushed and humble under her tread, and the smells of autumn condoled with her. Brewer the gardener, stamping out the ashes of his bonfire, saw her pass to and fro, a slender figure moving sedately between the unmoving boughs. He alone of all the household had taken his master's death without exclamation. Death coming to the old was a harmless thought to him, but looking at Laura he sighed deeply, as though he had planted her and now saw her dashed and broken by bad weather.

Ten days after Everard's death Henry and Caroline left Lady Place, taking Laura with them. She found the leave-taking less painful than she had expected, and Caroline put her to bed as soon as they arrived in Apsley Terrace, which simplified her unhappiness by making her feel like an unhappy child.

Laura had heard the others agreeing that the move to London would make her feel very differently. She had thought them stupid to suppose that any outward change could alter her mood. She now found that they had judged better than she. In Somerset she had grieved over her father's death. In London her grief was retracted into sudden realisations of her loss. She had thought that sorrow would be her companion for many years, and had planned for its entertainment. Now it visited her like sudden snow-storms, a hastening darkness across the sky, a transient whiteness and rigour cast upon her. She tried to recover the sentiment of renunciation which she had worn like a veil. It was gone, and gone with it was her sense of the dignity of bereavement.

Henry and Caroline did all they could to prevent her feeling unhappy. If they had been overlooking some shame of hers they could not have been more tactful, more modulatory. The first winter passed by like a half-frozen stream. At the turn of the year it grew extremely cold. Red cotton sandbags were laid along the window-sashes, and Fancy and Marion skated on the Round Pond with small astrakhan muffs. Laura did not skate, but she walked briskly along the path with Caroline, listening to the rock and jar of the skates grinding upon the ice and to the cries of the gulls overhead. She found London much colder than the country, though Henry assured her that this was impossible. She developed chilblains, and this annoyed her, for she had not had chilblains since she was a child. Then Nannie Quantrell would send her out in the early morning to run barefoot over the rimy lawn. There was a small garden at Apsley Terrace, but it had been gravelled over because Henry disliked the quality of London grass; and in any case it was not the sort of garden in which she could run barefoot.

She was also annoyed by the hardness of the London water. Her hands were so thin that they were always a little red; now they were rough also. If they could have remained idle, she would not have minded this so much. But Caroline never sat with idle hands; she would knit, or darn, or do useful needlework. Laura could not sit opposite her and do nothing. There was no useful needlework for her to do, Caroline did it all, so Laura was driven to embroidery. Each time that a strand of silk rasped against her fingers she shuddered inwardly.

Time went faster than the embroidery did. She had actually a sensation that she was stitching herself into a piece of embroidery with a good deal of background. But, as Caroline said, it was not possible to feel dull when there was so much to do. Indeed, it was surprising how much there was to do, and for everybody in the house. Even Laura, introduced as a sort of extra wheel, soon found herself part of the mechanism, and, interworking with the other wheels, went round as busily as they.

When she awoke, the day was already begun. She could hear iron noises from the kitchen, the sound of yesterday's ashes being probed out. Then came a smell of wood smoke – the kitchen fire had been laid anew and kindled in the cleansed grate. This was followed by the automatic noise of the carpet-sweeper and, breaking in upon it, the irregular knocking of the staircase brush against the banisters. The maid who brought her morning tea and laid the folded towel across the hot-water can had an experienced look; when she drew back the curtains she looked out upon the day with no curiosity. She had seen it already.

By the time the Willowes family met at breakfast all this activity had disappeared like the tide from the smooth, garnished beach. For the rest of the day it functioned unnoticed. Bells were answered, meals were served, all that appeared was completion. Yet unseen and underground the preparation and demolition of every day went on, like the inward persistent workings of heart and entrails. Sometimes a crash, a banging door, a voice upraised, would rend the veil of impersonality. And sometimes a sound of running water at unusual hours and a faint steaminess in the upper parts of the house betokened that one of the servants was having a bath.

After breakfast, and after Henry had been seen off, Caroline descended to the kitchen and Laura read the relinquished Times. Then came shopping, letter-writing, arranging the flowers, cleaning the canary-cage, and the girls' walk. Such things as arranging flowers or cleaning the canary-cage were done with a kind of precautions routine which made them seem alike solemn and illicit. The flowers were always arranged in the ground-floor lavatory, where there was a small sink; vases and wire frames were kept in a cupboard, and a pair of scissors was strung to a nail. Then the completed affair was carried carefully past the coats that hung in the lobby outside and set down upon some established site.

Every Tuesday the books were changed at the library.

After lunch there was a spell of embroidery and more Times. If it was fine, Caroline paid calls; if wet, she sat at home on the chance of receiving them. On Saturday afternoons there was the girls' dancing-class. Laura accompanied her nieces thither, carrying their slippers in a bag. She sat among the other parents and guardians upon a dais which shook to the primary accents of the pianist, watching lancers and polkas and waltzes being performed, and hearing Miss Parley say: 'Now we will recommence.' After the dancing was over there was a March of Grace, and when Fancy and Marion had miscarried of their curtseys she would envelop their muslin dresses and their red elbows in the grey ulsters, and walk them briskly home again.

They were dull children, though their dullness did not prevent them having a penetrating flow of conversation. Their ways and thoughts were governed by a sort of zodiacal procession of other little girls, and when they came down to the drawing-room after tea it seemed to Laura that they brought the Wardours, or the Wilkinsons, or the de la Bottes with them.

Dinner was at half-past seven. It was a sensible rule of Caroline's that at dinner only general topics should be discussed. The difficulties of the day (if the day had presented difficulties) were laid aside. To this rule Caroline attributed the excellence of Henry's digestion. Henry's digestion was further safeguarded by being left to itself in the smoking-room for an hour after dinner. If he was busy, this hour of meditation would be followed by some law-work. If not, he would join them in the drawing-room, or go to his club. When they were thus left by themselves Laura and Caroline went off to bed early, for they were pleasantly fatigued by their regular days and regular meals. Later on Laura, half asleep, would hear Henry's return from his club. The thud of the front door pulled to after him drove through the silent house, and this was followed by the noise of bolts and chains. Then the house, emptied of another day, creaked once or twice, and fell into repose, its silence and security barred up within it like a kind of moral family plate. The remainder of the night was left at the disposal of the grandfather's clock in the hall, equitably dealing out minutes and quarters and hours.

On Sunday mornings Henry would wind the clock. First one and then the other the quivering chains were wound up, till only the snouts of the leaden weights were visible, drooping sullenly over the abyss of time wherein they were to make their descent during the seven days following. After that the family went to church, and there were wound up for the week in much the same manner. They went to evening service too, but evening service was less austere. The vindictive sentiments sounded less vindictive; if an umbrella fell down with a crash the ensuing silence was less affronted; the sermon was shorter, or seemed so, and swung more robustly into 'And now to God the Father.'

After evening service came cold supper. Fancy and Marion sat up for this, and it was rather a cheerful meal, with extra trivialities such as sardines and celery. The leaden weights had already started upon their downward course.

Caroline was a religious woman. Resolute, orderly and unromantic, she would have made an admirable Mother Superior. In her housekeeping and her scrupulous account-books she expressed an almost mystical sense of the validity of small things. But like most true mystics, she was unsympathetic and difficult of approach. Once only did she speak her spiritual mind to Laura. Laura was nursing her when she had influenza; Caroline wished to put on a clean nightdress, and Laura, opening the third drawer of the large mahogany wardrobe, had commented upon the beautiful orderliness with which Caroline's body linen was arranged therein. 'We have our example,' said Caroline. 'The graveclothes were folded in the tomb.'

Looking into the large shadowy drawer, where nightgowns and chemises lay folded exactly upon each other in a purity that disdained even lavender, Laura shuddered a little at this revelation of her sister-in-law's private thoughts. She made no answer, and never again did Caroline open her mind to her upon such matters.

Laura never forgot this. Caroline seemed affectionately disposed towards her; she was full of practical good sense, her advice was excellent, and pleasantly bestowed. Laura saw her a good wife, a fond and discreet mother, a kind mistress, a most conscientious sister-in-law. She was also rather gluttonous. But for none of these qualities could Laura feel at ease with her. Compared to Caroline she knew herself to be unpractical, unmethodical, lacking in initiative. The tasks that Caroline delegated to her she performed eagerly and carefully, but she performed them with the hampering consciousness that Caroline could do them better than she, and in less time. Even in so simple a matter as holding a skein of wool for Caroline to wind off into a ball, Caroline's large white fingers worked so swiftly that it was she who twitched the next length off Laura's thumb before Laura, watching the diminishing thread, remembered to dip her hand. But all this – for Laura was humble and Caroline kind – could have been overcome. It was in the things that never appeared that Laura felt her inadequacy.

Laura was not in any way religious. She was not even religious enough to speculate towards irréligion. She went with Caroline to early service whenever Caroline's inquiries suggested it, and to morning service and evening service every Sunday; she knelt beside her and heard her pray in a small, stilled version of the voice which she knew so well in its clear everyday ordinances. Religion was great-great-aunt Salome's prayer-book which Caroline held in her gloved hands. Religion was a strand in the Willowes' life, and the prayer-book was the outward sign of it. But it was also the outward sign of the puff pastry which had been praised by King George in. Religion was something to be preserved: it was part of the Willowes life and so was the prayer-book, preserved from generation to generation.

Laura was bored by the church which they attended. She would have liked, now that she was come to London, to see the world, to adventure in churches. She was darkly, adventurously drawn to see what services were like amongst Roman Catholics, amongst Huguenots, amongst Unitarians and Swedenborgians, feeling about this rather as she felt about the East End. She expressed her wish to Caroline, and Caroline, rather unexpectedly, had been inclined to further it. But Henry banned the project. It would not do for Laura to go elsewhere than to the family place of worship, he said. For Henry, the family place of worship was the pew upon whose ledge rested great-great-aunt Salome's prayer-book. He felt this less explicitly than the straying Laura did, for he was a man and had less time to think of such things. But he felt it strongly.

Laura believed that she would like Caroline if she could only understand her She had no difficulty in understanding Henry, but for no amount of understanding could she much like him. After some years in his house she came to the conclusion that Caroline had been very bad for his character. Caroline was a good woman and a good wife. She was slightly self-righteous, and fairly rightly so, but she yielded to Henry's judgment in every dispute, she bowed her good sense to his will and blinkered her wider views in obedience to his prejudices. Henry had a high opinion of her merits, but thinking her to be so admirable and finding her to be so acquiescent had encouraged him to have an even higher opinion of his own. However good a wife Caroline might choose to be, she could not quite make Henry a bad husband or a bad man – he was too much of a Willowes for that: but she fed his vanity, and ministered to his imperiousness.

Laura also thought that the law had done a great deal to spoil Henry. It had changed his natural sturdy stupidity into a browbeating indifference to other people's point of view. He seemed to consider himself briefed by his Creator to turn into ridicule the opinions of those who disagreed with him, and to attribute dishonesty, idiocy, or a base motive to everyone who supported a better case than he. This did not often appear in his private life, Henry was kindly disposed to those who did not thwart him by word or deed. His household had been well schooled by Caroline in yielding gracefully, and she was careful not to invite guests who were not of her husband's way of thinking.

Most of their acquaintance were people connected with the law. Laura grew familiar with the legal manner, but she did not grow fond of it. She felt that these clean-shaven men with bristling eyebrows were suavely concealing their doubts of her intelligence and her probity. Their jaws were like so many mousetraps, baited with commonplaces. They made her feel shy and behave stiffly.

This was unfortunate, as Henry and Caroline had hoped that some one of them would fall sufficiently in love with Laura to marry her. Mr. Fortescue, Mr. Parker, Mr. Jermyn, Mr. Danby, Mr. Thrush, were in turn selected as suitable and likely undertakers. Every decent effort was made by Henry and Caroline, and a certain number of efforts were made by the chosen. But Laura would make no efforts at all. Henry and Caroline had lost heart when they invited Mr. Arbuthnot to tea on Sunday. They invited him for pity's sake, and but to tea at that, for he was very shy and stammered. To their surprise they saw Laura taking special pains to be nice to him. Equally to their surprise they saw Mr. Arbuthnot laying aside his special pains to observe a legal manner and stammering away quite enthusiastically about climbing Welsh mountains and gathering parsley fern. They scarcely dared to hope, for they felt the time for hope was gone by. However, they invited him to dinner, and did their best to be on friendly terms with him.

Mr. Arbuthnot received their advances without surprise, for he had a very good opinion of himself. He felt that being thirty-five he owed himself a wife, and he also felt that Laura would do very nicely. His aunt, Lady Ross-Price, always tried to get servants from the Willowes establishment, for Mrs. Willowes trained them so well. Mr. Arbuthnot supposed that Mrs. Willowes would be equally good at training wives. He began to think of Laura quite tenderly, and Caroline began to read the Stores' catalogue quite seriously. This was the moment when Laura, who had been behaving nicely for years, chose to indulge her fantasy, and to wreck in five minutes the good intentions of as many months.

She had come more and more to look on Mr. Arbuthnot as an indulgence. His stammer had endeared him to her; it seemed, after so much legal manner, quite sympathetic. Though nothing would have induced her to marry him, she was very ready to talk to him, and even to talk naturally of what came uppermost in her thoughts. Laura's thoughts ranged over a wide field, even now. Sometimes she said rather amusing things, and displayed unexpected stores (General Stores) of knowledge. But her remarks were as a rule so disconnected from the conversation that no one paid much attention to them. Mr. Arbuthnot certainly was not prepared for her response to his statement that February was a dangerous month. 'It is,' answered Laura with almost violent agreement. 'If you are a wire-wolf, and very likely you may be, for lots of people are without knowing, February, of all months, is the month when you are most likely to go out on a dark windy night and worry sheep.'

Henry and Caroline glanced at each other in horror. Mr. Arbuthnot said: 'How very interesting! But I really don't think I am likely to do such a thing.' Laura made no answer. She did not think so either. But she was amusing herself with a surprisingly vivid and terrible picture of Mr. Arbuthnot cloaked in a shaggy hide and going with heavy devouring swiftness upon all-fours with a lamb dangling from his mouth.

This settled it. Henry and Caroline made no more attempts to marry off Laura. Trying to do so had been a nuisance and an expense, and Laura had never shown the smallest appreciation of their trouble. Before long they would have the girls to think of. Fancy was sixteen, and Marion nearly as tall as Fancy. In two years they would have to begin again. They were glad of a respite, and made the most of it. Laura also was glad of a respite. She bought second-hand copies of Herodotus and Johnson's Dictionary to read in the evenings. Caroline, still sewing on buttons, would look at her sister-in-law's composed profile. Laura's hair was black as ever, but it was not so thick. She had grown paler from living in London. Her forehead had not a wrinkle, but two downward lines prolonged the drooping corners of her mouth. Her face was beginning to stiffen. It had lost its power of expressiveness, and was more and more dominated by the hook nose and the sharp chin. When Laura was ten years older she would be nut-crackerish.

Caroline resigned herself to spending the rest of her evenings with Laura beside her. The perpetual company of a sister-in-law was rather more than she had bargained for. Still, there she was, and Henry was right – they had been the proper people to make a home for Laura when her father died, and she was too old now to begin living by herself. It was not as if she had had any experience of life; she had passed from one guardianship to another: it was impossible to imagine Laura fending for herself. A kind of pity for the unused virgin beside her spread through Caroline's thoughts. She did not attach an inordinate value to her wifehood and maternity; they were her duties, rather than her glories. But for all that she felt emotionally plumper than Laura. It was well to be loved, to be necessary to other people. But Laura too was loved, and Laura was necessary. Caroline did not know what the children would do without their Aunt Lolly.

Every one spoke of her as Aunt Lolly, till in the course of time she had almost forgotten her baptismal name.

'Say How-do to Auntie Laura,' said Caroline to Fancy. This was long ago in the re-furbished nursery at Lady Place where Laura knelt timidly before her first niece, while the London nurse bustled round them unpacking soft hairbrushes and pots of cold cream, and hanging linen to air upon the tall nursery fender.

'How-do, Auntie Lolly,' said Fancy, graciously thrusting forward a fur monkey.

'She's taken to you at once, Laura,' said Caroline. 'I was afraid this journey would upset her, but she's borne it better than any of us.'

'Journeys are nothing to them at that age, ma'am,' said the nurse. 'Now suppose you tell your new auntie what you call Monkey.'

'Auntie Lolly, Auntie Lolly,' repeated Fancy, rhythmically banging the monkey against the table-leg.

The name hit upon by Fancy was accepted by Marion and Titus; before long their parents made use of it also. Everard never spoke of his daughter but as Laura, even when he spoke of her to his grandchildren. He was too old to change his ways, and he had, in any case, a prejudice against nicknames and abbreviations. But when Laura went to London she left Laura behind, and entered into a state of Aunt Lolly. She had quitted so much of herself in quitting Somerset that it seemed natural to relinquish her name also. Divested of her easily-worn honours as mistress of the household, shorn of her long meandering country days, sleeping in a smart brass bedstead instead of her old and rather pompous four-poster, wearing unaccustomed clothes and performing unaccustomed duties, she seemed to herself to have become a different person. Or rather, she had become two persons, each different. One was Aunt Lolly, a middleaging lady, light-footed upon stairs, and indispensable for Christmas Eve and birthday preparations. The other was Miss Willowes, 'my sister-in-law Miss Willowes,' whom Caroline would introduce, and abandon to a feeling of being neither light-footed nor indispensable. But Laura was put away. When Henry asked her to witness some document for him her Laura Erminia Willowes seemed as much a thing out of common speech as the Spinster that followed it. She would look, and be surprised that such a dignified name should belong to her.

Twice a year, in spring and in summer, the Willowes family went into the country for a holiday. For the first three years of Laura's London life they went as a matter of course to Lady Place. There once more arose the problem of how two children of one sex can play nicely with a much younger child of the other. Fancy and Marion played at tea-parties under the weeping ash, and Titus was the butler with a tin tray. Titus would presently run off and play by himself at soldiers, beating martial tattoos upon the tray. But now there was no danger of the youngest member of the party falling into the pond, for Aunt Lolly was always on guard.

Laura enjoyed the visits to Lady Place, but her enjoyment did not go very deep. The knowledge that she was now a visitor where she had formerly been at home seemed to place a clear sheet of glass between her and her surroundings. She felt none of the grudge of the dispossessed; she scarcely gave a thought to the old days. It was as if in the agony of leaving Lady Place after her father's death she had said good-bye so irremediably that she could never really come there again.

But the visits to Lady Place came to a sad end, for in 1905 James died suddenly of heartfailure. Sibyl decided that she could not go on living alone in the country. A manager was found for the brewery, Lady Place was let unfurnished upon a long lease, and Sibyl and the four-years-old heir of the Willowes name and traditions moved to a small house in Hampstead. Sibyl had proposed to sell some of the furniture, for there was a great deal more of it than she needed, and most of it was too large to fit into her new dwelling. This project was opposed by Henry, and with considerable heat. The family establishment must, he admitted, be broken up, but he would allow no part of it to be alienated. All the furniture that could not be found room for at Hampstead or at Apsley Terrace must be stored till Titus should be of an age to resume the tenure of Lady Place.

To Laura it seemed as though some familiar murmuring brook had suddenly gone underground. There it flowed, silenced and obscured, until the moment when it should reappear and murmur again between green banks. She thought of Titus as a grown man and herself as an old woman meeting among the familiar belongings. She believed that when she was told the ghost-like feeling that distressed her would matter less. She hoped that she might not die before that day, if it were only that she would remember so well, as Titus could not, how the furniture stood in the rooms and the pictures hung on the walls.

But by then, she said to herself, Titus would have a wife with tastes of her own. Sibyl would have liked to alter several things, but tradition had been too strong for her. It would be a very different matter in twenty years' time. The chairs and tables and cabinets would come out blinking and forgetful from their long storage in darkness. They would have lost the individuality by which they had made certain corners so surely their own. The Lady Place she had known was over. She could remember it if she pleased; but she must not think of it.

Meanwhile Emma's harp trailed its strings in her bedroom. Ratafee was removed to Hampstead. Titus had insisted upon this.

She wondered if Henry felt as she did. He had shown a great deal of Willowes spirit over the furniture, but otherwise he had not expressed himself In person Henry, so it was said, resembled his grandfather who had made the move from Dorset to Somerset – the sacrilegious move which the home-loving of the Willoweses had so soon sanctified that in the third generation she was feeling like this about Lady Place. Henry seemed to resemble his grandfather in spirit also. He could house all the family traditions in his practical mind, and for the rest talk about bricks and mortar. He concerned himself with the terms of Sibyl's lease, the agreement with the manager of the brewery, and the question of finding a satisfactory place to carry his family to for the holidays.

After some experiments they settled down to a routine that with a few modifications for the sake of variety or convenience served them for the next fifteen years. In spring they went to some moderately popular health resort and stayed in a hotel, for it was found that the uncertainty of an English spring, let alone the uncertainty of a Christian Easter, made lodgings unsatisfactory at that time of year. In summer they went into lodgings, or took a furnished house in some seaside village without any attractions.

They did this, not to be economical – there was no need for economy – but because they found rather plain dull holidays the most refreshing Henry was content with a little unsophisticated golf and float-fishing. The children bathed and played on the beach and went on bicycling expeditions; and Caroline and Laura watched the children bathe and play, and replenished their stock of underclothes, and rested from the strain of London housekeeping. Sometimes Caroline did a little reading. Sometimes Sibyl and Titus stayed with them, or Titus stayed with them alone while his mother paid visits.

Laura looked forward with pleasure to the summer holidays (the Easter holidays she never cared about, as she had a particular dislike for palms); but after the first shock of arrival and smelling the sea, the days seemed to dribble out very much like the days in London. When the end came, and she looked back from the wagonette over the past weeks, she found that after all she had done few of the things she intended to do. She would have liked to go by herself for long walks inland and find strange herbs, but she was too useful to be allowed to stray. She had once formed an indistinct project of observing limpets. But for all her observations she discovered little save that if you sit very still for a long time the limpet will begin to move sideways, and that it is almost impossible to sit very still for a long time and keep your attention fixed upon such a small object as a limpet without feeling slightly hypnotised and slightly sick. On the lowest count she seldom contrived to read all the books or to finish all the needlework which she had taken with her. And the freckles on her nose mocked her with the receptivity of her skin compared to the dullness of her senses.

They were submerged in the usual quiet summer holidays when the war broke out. The parish magazine said: 'The vicar had scarcely left East Bingham when war was declared.' The vicar was made of stouter stuff than they. He continued his holiday, but the Willoweses went back to London. Laura had never seen London in August before. It had an arrested look, as though the war were a kind of premature autumn. She was extraordinarily moved; as they drove across the river from Waterloo she wanted to cry. That same evening Fancy went upstairs and scrubbed the boxroom floor for the sake of practice. She upset the bucket, and large damp patches appeared on the ceiling of Laura's room.

For a month Fancy behaved like a cat whose kittens have been drowned. If her family had not been so taken up with the war they would have been alarmed at this change in her demeanour. As it was, they scarcely noticed it. When she came in very late for lunch and said: 'I am going to marry Kit Bendigo on Saturday,' Henry said, 'Very well, my dear. It's your day, not mine,' and ordered champagne to be brought up. For a moment Laura thought she heard her father speaking. She knew that Henry disapproved of Kit Bendigo as a husband for Fancy: Willoweses did not mate with Bendigos. But now he was more than resigned – he was ready. And he swallowed the gnat as unswervingly as the camel, which, if Laura had wanted to be ill-natured just then, would have surprised her as being the greater feat Willoweses do not marry at five days' notice. But Fancy was married on Saturday, and her parents discovered that a hasty wedding can cost quite as much as a formal one. In the mood that they were in this afforded them some slight satisfaction.

Kit Bendigo was killed in December 1916. Fancy received the news calmly; two years' warwork and a daughter thrown in had steadied her nerves. Kit was a dear, of course, poor old Kit But there was a war on, and people get killed in wars. If it came to that, she was working in a high-explosive shed herself. Caroline could not understand her eldest daughter. She was baffled and annoyed by the turn her own good sense inherited had taken. The married nun looked at the widowed amazon and refused battle. At least Fancy might stay in her very expensive flat and be a mother to her baby. But Fancy drew on a pair of heavy gauntlet gloves and went to France to drive motor lorries. Caroline dared not say a word.

The war had no such excitements for Laura. Four times a week she went to a depot and did up parcels. She did them up so well that no one thought of offering her a change of work. The parcel-room was cold and encumbered, early in the war someone had decorated the walls with recruiting posters. By degrees these faded. The ruddy young man and his Spartan mother grew pale, as if with fear, and Britannia's scarlet cloak trailing on the waters bleached to a cocoa-ish pink. Laura watched them discolour with a muffled heart. She would not allow herself the cheap symbolism they provoked. Time will bleach the scarlet from young men's cheeks, and from Britannia's mantle. But blood was scarlet as ever, and she believed that, however despairing her disapproval, that blood was being shed for her.

She continued to do up parcels until the eleventh day of November 1918. Then, when she heard the noise of cheering and the sounding of hooters, she left her work and went home. The house was empty. Everyone had gone out to rejoice. She went up to her room and sat down on the bed. She felt cold and sick, she trembled from head to foot as once she had done after witnessing a dog-fight. All the hooters were sounding, they seemed to domineer over the noises of rejoicing with sarcastic emphasis. She got up and walked about the room. On the mantelpiece was a photograph of Titus. 'Well,' she said to it, 'you've escaped killing, anyhow.' Her voice sounded harsh and unreal, she thought the walls of her room were shaking at the concussion, like stage walls. She lay down upon her bed, and presently fainted.

When she came to herself again she had been discovered by Caroline and put to bed with influenza. She was grateful for this, and for the darkened room and the cool clinking tumblers. She was even grateful for the bad dreams which visited her every night and sent up her tempera-ture. By their aid she was enabled to stay in bed for a fortnight, a thing she had not done since she came to London.

When she went downstairs again she found Henry and Caroline talking of better days to come. The house was unaltered, yet it had a general air of refurbishment. She also, after her fortnight in bed, felt somehow refurbished, and was soon drawn into the talk of better days. There was nothing immoderate in the family display of satisfaction. Henry still found frowning matter in the Times, and Caroline did not relinquish a single economy. But the satisfaction was there, a demure Willowes-like satisfaction in the family tree that had endured the gale with an unflinching green heart. Laura saw nothing in this to quarrel with. She was rather proud of the Willowes war record; she admired the stolid decorum which had mastered four years of disintegration, and was stolid and decorous still. A lady had inquired of Henry: 'What do you do in air-raids? Do you go down to the cellar or up to the roof?' 'We do neither,' Henry had replied. 'We stay where we are.' A thrill had passed through Laura when she heard this statement of the Willowes mind. But afterwards she questioned the validity of the thrill. Was it nothing more than the response of her emotions to other old and honourable symbols such as the trooping of the colours and the fifteenth chapter of Corinthians, symbols too old and too honourable to have called out her thoughts? She saw how admirable it was for Henry and Caroline to have stayed where they were. But she was conscious, more conscious than they were, that the younger members of the family had somehow moved into new positions. And she herself, had she not slightly strained against her moorings, fast and far sunk as they were? But now the buffeting waves withdrew, and she began to settle back into her place, and to see all around her once more the familiar undisturbed shadows of familiar things. Outwardly there was no difference between her and Henry and Caroline in their resumption of peace. But they, she thought, had done with the war, whereas she had only shelved it, and that by an accident of consciousness.

When the better days to come came, they proved to be modelled as closely as possible upon the days that were past. It was astonishing what little difference differences had made. When they went back to East Bingham – for owing to its military importance, East Bingham had been unsuited for holidays – there were at first a good many traces of war lying about, such as sandbags and barbed-wire entanglements. But on the following summer the sandbags had rotted and burst and the barbed-wire had been absorbed into the farmer's fences. So, Laura thought, such warlike phenomena as Mr. Wolf-Saunders, Fancy's second husband, and Jemima and Rosalind, Fancy's two daughters, might well disappear off the family landscape.

Mr. Wolf-Saunders recumbent on the beach was indeed much like a sandbag, and no more arresting to the eye. Jemima and Rosalind were more obtrusive. Here was a new generation to call her Aunt Lolly and find her as indispensable as did the last.

'It is quite like old times,' said Caroline, who sat working beside her. 'Isn't it, Lolly?'

'Except for these anachronisms,' said Laura.

Caroline removed the seaweed which Jemima had stuffed into her work-bag. 'Bless them!' she said absently. 'We shall soon be back in town again.'

PART II

The Willoweses came back to London about the second week in September. For many years the children's schooling had governed the date of their return; and when the children had grown too old for school, the habit had grown too old to be broken. There was also a further reason. The fallen leaves, so Henry and Caroline thought, made the country unhealthy after the second week in September. When Laura was younger she had sometimes tried to argue that, even allowing the unhealthiness of fallen leaves, leaves at that time of year were still green upon the trees. This was considered mere casuistry. When they walked in Kensington Gardens upon the first Sunday morning after their return, Caroline would point along the tarnishing vistas and say: 'You see, Lolly, the leaves are beginning to fall. It was quite time to come home.'

It was useless to protest that autumn begins earlier in London than it does in the country. That it did so, Laura knew well. That was why she disliked having to come back; autumn boded her no good, and it was hard that by a day's train-journey she should lose almost a month's reprieve. Obediently looking along the tarnishing vistas, she knew that once again she was in for it. What It was exactly, she would have found hard to say. She sometimes told herself that it must be the yearly reverberation of those miserable first months in London when her sorrow for her father's death was still fresh. No other winter had been so cold or so long, not even the long cold winters of the war. Yet now her thoughts of Everard were mellowed and painless, and she had long ago forgiven her sorrow. Had the coming of autumn quickened in her only an experienced grief she would not have dreaded it thus, nor felt so restless and tormented. Her disquiet had no relevance to her life. It arose out of the ground with the smell of the dead leaves: it followed her through the darkening streets; it confronted her in the look of the risen moon. 'Now! Now!' it said to her: and no more. The moon seemed to have torn the leaves from the trees that it might stare at her more imperiously. Sometimes she tried to account for her uneasiness by saying that she was growing old, and that the year's death reminded her of her own. She compared herself to the ripening acorn that feels through windless autumnal days and nights the increasing pull of the earth below. That explanation was very poetical and suitable. But it did not explain what she felt She was not wildly anxious either to die or to live; why, then, should she be rent by this anxiety?

At these times she was subject to a peculiar kind of day-dreaming, so vivid as to be almost a hallucination: that she was in the country, at dusk, and alone, and strangely at peace. She did not recall the places which she had visited in holiday-time, these reproached her like opportunities neglected. But while her body sat before the first fires and was cosy with Henry and Caroline, her mind walked by lonely sea-bords, in marshes and fens, or came at nightfall to the edge of a wood. She never imagined herself in these places by daylight. She never thought of them as being in any way beautiful. It was not beauty at all that she wanted, or, depressed though she was, she would have bought a ticket to somewhere or other upon the Metropolitan railway and gone out to see the recumbent autumnal graces of the country-side. Her mind was groping after something that eluded her experience, a something that was shadowy and menacing, and yet in some way congenial; a something that lurked in waste places, that was hinted at by the sound of water gurgling through deep channels and by the voices of birds of ill-omen. Loneliness, dreariness, aptness for arousing a sense of fear, a kind of ungodly hallowedness – these were the things that called her thoughts away from the comfortable fireside.

In this mood she would sometimes go off to explore among the City churches, or to lose herself in the riverside quarters east of the Pool. She liked to think of the London of Defoe's Journal, and to fancy herself back in the seventeenth century, when, so it seemed to her, there were still darknesses in men's minds. Once, hemmed in by the jostling tombstones at Bunhill Fields, she almost pounced on the clue to her disquiet; and once again in the goods-yard of the G.W.R., where she had gone to find, not her own secret, but a case of apples for Caroline.

As time went on Laura grew accustomed to this recurrent autumnal fever. It was as much a sign of the season as the falling leaves or the first frost. Before the end of November it was all over and done with. The next moon had no message for her. Her rambles in the strange places of the mind were at an end. And if she still went on expeditions to Rotherhithe or the Jews' Burying-Ground, she went in search for no more than a little diversion.

Nothing was left but cold and sleet and the knowledge that all this fuss had been about nothing. She fortified herself against the dismalness of this reaction by various small self-indulgences. Out of these she had contrived for herself a sort of mental fur coat. Roasted chestnuts could be bought and taken home for bedroom eating. Second-hand book-shops were never so enticing; and the combination of east winds and London water made it allowable to experiment in the most expensive soaps. Coming back from her expeditions, westward from the city with the sunset in her eyes, or eastward from a waning Kew, she would pause for a sumptuous and furtive tea, eating marrons glacés with a silver fork in the reflecting warm glitter of a smart pastry-cook's These things were exciting enough to be pleasurable, for she kept them secret. Henry and Caroline would scarcely have minded if they had known. They were quite indifferent as to where and how she spent her afternoons; they felt no need to question her, since they could be sure that she would do nothing unsuitable or extravagant. Laura's expeditions were secret because no one asked her where she had been. Had they asked, she must have answered. But she did not examine too closely into this; she liked to think of them as secret.

One manifestation of the fur-coat policy, however, could not be kept from their knowledge, and that manifestation slightly qualified their trust that Laura would do nothing unsuitable or extravagant.

Except for a gradual increment of Christmas and birthday presents, Laura's room had altered little since the day it ceased to be the small spare-room and became hers. But every winter it blossomed with an unseasonable luxury of flowers, profusely, shameless as a greenhouse. 'Why, Lolly! Lilies at this time of year!'

Caroline would say, not reproachfully, but still with a consciousness that in the drawing-room there were dahlias, and in the dining-room a fern, and in her own sitting-room, where she did the accounts, neither ferns nor flowers. Then Laura would thrust the lilies into her hands; and she would take them to show that she had not spoken with ill-will. Besides, Lolly would really see more of them if they were in the drawing-room. And the next day she would meet Laura on the stairs carrying azaleas. On one occasion even Henry had noticed the splendour of the lilies: red lilies, angular, authoritative in form and colour like cardinal's hats.

'Where do these come from?' Caroline had asked, knowing well that nothing so costly in appearance could come from her florist.

'From Africa,' Laura had answered, pressing the firm, wet stalks into her hand.

'Oh well, I daresay they are quite common flowers there,' said Caroline to herself, trying to gloss over the slight awkwardness of accepting a trifle so needlessly splendid.

Henry had also asked where they came from.

'From Anthos, I believe,' said Caroline.

'Ah!' said Henry, and roused the coins in his trousers pocket.

'It's rather naughty of Lolly. Would you like me just to hint to her that she mustn't be quite so reckless?'

'No. Better not. No need for her to worry about such things.'

Husband and wife exchanged a glance of compassionate understanding. It was better not. Much better that Lolly should not be worried about money matters. She was safe in their hands. They could look after Lolly. Henry was like a wall, and Caroline's breasts were like towers.

They condoned this extravagance, yet they mistrusted it. Time justified them in their mistrust. Like many stupid people, they possessed acute instincts. 'He that is unfaithful in little things...' Caroline would say when the children forgot to wind up their watches. Their instinct told them that the same truth applies to extravagance in little things. They were wiser than they knew. When Laura's extravagance in great things came it staggered them so completely that they forgot how judiciously they had suspected it beforehand.

It befell in the winter of 1921. The war was safely over, so was their silver wedding, so was Marion's first confinement. Titus was in his third year at Oxford, Sibyl was at last going grey, Henry might be made a judge at any moment. The Trade Returns and the Stock Exchange were not all that they should be, and there was always the influenza. But Henry was doing well enough to be lenient to his investments, and Aunt Lucilla and her fortune had been mercifully released. In the coming spring Caroline proposed to have the house thoroughly done up. The lesser renovations she was getting over beforehand, and that was why Laura had gone out before the shops shut to show Mr. Bunting a pair of massy candlesticks and to inquire how much he would charge for re-plating them. His estimate was high, too high to be accepted upon her own responsibility. She decided to carry the candlesticks back and consult Caroline.

Mr. Bunting lived in the Earls Court Road, rather a long way off for such a family friend. But she had plenty of time for walking back, and for diversion she thought she would take a circuitous route, including the two foxes who guard the forsaken approach in Holland Park and the lane beside the Bayswater Synagogue. It was in Moscow Road that she began to be extravagant. But when she walked into the little shop she had no particular intention of extravagance, for Caroline's parcel hung re-mindingly upon her arm, and the shop itself, half florist and half greengrocer, had a simple appearance.

There were several other customers, and while she stood waiting to be served she looked about her. The aspect of the shop pleased her greatly. It was small and homely. Fruit and flowers and vegetables were crowded together in countrified disorder. On the sloping shelf in the window, among apples and rough-skinned cooking pears and trays of walnuts, chestnuts, and filberts, was a basket of eggs, smooth and brown, like some larger kind of nut. At one side of the room was a wooden staging. On this stood jars of home-made jam and bottled fruits. It was as though the remnants of summer had come into the little shop for shelter. On the floor lay a heap of earthy turnips.

Laura looked at the bottled fruits, the sliced pears in syrup, the glistening red plums, the greengages. She thought of the woman who had filled those jars and fastened on the bladders. Perhaps the greengrocer's mother lived in the country. A solitary old woman picking fruit in a darkening orchard, rubbing her rough fingertips over the smooth-skinned plums, a lean wiry old woman, standing with upstretched arms among her fruit trees as though she were a tree herself, growing out of the long grass, with arms stretched up like branches. It grew darker and darker; still she worked on, methodically stripping the quivering taut boughs one after the other.

As Laura stood waiting she felt a great longing It weighed upon her like the load of ripened fruit upon a tree. She forgot the shop, the other customers, her own errand. She forgot the winter air outside, the people going by on the wet pavements.

She forgot that she was in London, she forgot the whole of her London life. She seemed to be standing alone in a darkening orchard, her feet in the grass, her arms stretched up to the pattern of leaves and fruit, her fingers seeking the rounded ovals of the fruit among the pointed ovals of the leaves. The air about her was cool and moist. There was no sound, for the birds had left off singing and the owls had not yet begun to hoot. No sound, except sometimes the soft thud of a ripe plum falling into the grass, to lie there a compact shadow among shadows. The back of her neck ached a little with the strain of holding up her arms. Her fingers searched among the leaves.

She started as the man of the shop came up to her and asked her what she wished for. Her eyes blinked, she looked with surprise at the gloves upon her hands.

'I want one of those large chrysanthemums,' she said, and turned towards the window where they stood in a brown jar. There were the apples and pears, the eggs, the disordered nuts overflowing from their compartments. There on the floor were the earthy turnips, and close at hand were the jams and bottled fruits. If she was behaving foolishly, if she looked like a woman roused out of a fond dream, these were kindly things to waken to. The man of the shop also had a kind face. He wore a gardener's apron, and his hands were brown and dry as if he had been handling earth.

'Which one would you like, ma'am?' he asked, turning the bunch of chrysanthemums about that she might choose for herself. She looked at the large mop-headed blossoms. Their curled petals were deep garnet colour within and tawny yellow without. As the light fell on their sleek flesh the garnet colour glowed, the tawny yellow paled as if it were thinly washed with silver. She longed for the moment when she might stroke her hand over those mop heads.

'I think I will take them all,' she said.

'They're lovely blooms,' said the man.

He was pleased. He did not expect such a good customer at this late hour. When he brought her the change from her pound-note and the chrysanthemums pinned up in sheets of white paper, he brought also several sprays of beech leaves. These, he explained, were thrown in with her purchase. Laura took them into her arms. The great fans of orange tracery seemed to her even more beautiful than the chrysanthemums, for they had been given to her, they were a surprise. She sniffed. They smelt of woods, of dark rustling woods like the wood to whose edge she came so often in the country of her autumn imagination. She stood very still to make quite sure of her sensations. Then: 'Where do they come from?' she asked.

'From near Chenies, ma'am, in Buckinghamshire. I have a sister living there, and every Sunday I go out to see her, and bring back a load of foliage with me.'

There was no need to ask now who made the jams and tied on the bladders. Laura knew all that she wanted to know. Her course lay clear before her. Holding the sprays of beech as though she were marching on Dunsinane, she went to a bookseller's. There she bought a small guide-book to the Chilterns and inquired for a map of that district. It must, she explained, be very detailed, and give as many names and footpaths as possible. Her eyes were so bright and her demands so earnest that the bookseller, though he had not that kind of map, was sympathetic, and directed her to another shop where she could find what she wanted. It was only a little way off, but closing-time was at hand, so she took a taxi. Having bought the map she took another taxi home. But at the top of Apsley Terrace she had one of her impulses of secrecy and told the driver that she would walk the rest of the way.

There was rather a narrow squeak in the hall, for Caroline's parcel became entangled in the gong stand, and she heard Henry coming up from the wine cellar. If she alarmed the gong Henry would quicken his steps. She had no time to waste on Henry just then for she had a great deal to think of before dinner. She ran up to her room, arranged the chrysanthemums and the beech leaves, and began to read the guide-book. It was just what she wanted, for it was extremely plain and unperturbed. Beginning as early as possible with Geology, it passed to Flora and Fauna, Watersheds, Ecclesiastical Foundations and Local Government. After that came a list of all the towns and villages, shortly described in alphabetical order. Lamb's End had three hundred inhabitants and a perpendicular font. At Walpole St. Dennis was the country seat of the Bartlet family, faced with stucco and situated upon an eminence. The almshouses at Semple, built in 1703 by Bethia Hood, had a fine pair of wrought-iron gates. It was dark as she pressed her nose against the scrolls and rivets. Bats flickered in the little courtyard, and shadows moved across the yellow blinds. Had she been born a deserving widow, life would have been simplified.

She wasted no time over this regret, for now at last she was simplifying life for herself. She unfolded the map. The woods were coloured green and the main roads red. There was a great deal of green. She looked at the beech leaves. As she looked a leaf detached itself and fell slowly. She remembered squirrels.

The stairs creaked under the tread of Dunlop with the hot-water can. Dunlop entered, glancing neither at Laura curled askew on the bed nor at the chrysanthemums ennobling the dressing-table. She was a perfectly trained servant. Before she left the room she took a deep breath, stooped down, and picked up the beech leaf.

Quarter of an hour afterwards Laura exclaimed: 'Oh! a windmill!' She took up the guide-book again, and began to read intently.

She was roused by an unaccustomed clash of affable voices in the hall. She remembered, leapt off the bed, and dressed rapidly for the family dinner-party. They were all there when she reached the drawing-room. Sibyl and Titus, Fancy and her Mr. Wolf-Saunders, Marion with the latest news from Sprat, who, being in the Soudan, could not dine out with his wife. Sprat had had another boil on his neck, but it had yielded to treatment. 'Ah, poor fellow,' said Henry. He seemed to be saying: 'The price of Empire.'

During dinner Laura looked at her relations She felt as though she had awoken, unchanged, from a twenty-years slumber, to find them almost unrecognisable. She surveyed them, one after the other. Even Henry and Caroline, whom she saw every day, were half hidden under their accumulations – accumulations of prosperity, authority, daily experience. They were carpeted with experience. No new event could set jarring foot on them but they would absorb and muffle the impact. If the boiler burst, if a policeman climbed in at the window waving a sword, Henry and Caroline would bring the situation to heel by their massive experience of normal boilers and normal policemen. She turned her eyes to Sibyl. How strange it was that Sibyl should have exchanged her former look of a pretty ferret for this refined and waxen mask. Only when she was silent, though, as now she was, listening to Henry with her eyes cast down to her empty plate: when she spoke the ferret look came back. But Sibyl in her house at Hampstead must have spent many long afternoons in silence, learning this unexpected beauty, preparing her face for the last look of death. What had been her thoughts? Why was she so different when she spoke? Which, what, was the real Sibyl: the greedy, agile little ferret or this memorial urn?

Fancy's Mr. Wolf-Saunders had eaten all his bread and was at a loss. Laura turned to him and asked after her great-nephew, who was just then determined to be a bus-conductor. 'He probably will be,' said his father gloomily, 'if things go on as they are at present.'

Great-nephews and great-nieces suggested nephews and nieces. Resuming her scrutiny of the table she looked at Fancy, Marion, and Titus. They had grown up as surprisingly as trees since she first knew them, and yet it did not seem to her that they were so much changed as their elders. Titus, in particular, was easily recognisable. She caught his eye, and he smiled back at her, just as he had smiled back when he was a baby. Now he was long and slim, and his hay-coloured hair was brushed smoothly back instead of standing up in a crest. But one lock had fallen forward when he laughed, and hung over his left eye, and this gave him a pleasing, rustic look. She was glad still to be friends with Titus. He might very usefully abet her, and though she felt in no need of allies, a little sympathy would do no harm. Certainly the rustic forelock made Titus look particularly congenial. And how greedily he was eating that apple, and with what disparagement of imported fruit he had waved away the Californian plums! It was nice to feel sure of his understanding and approval, since at this moment he was looking the greatest Willowes of them all.

Most of the family attention was focussed on Titus that evening. No sooner had coffee been served than Sibyl began about his career Had Caroline ever heard of anything more ridiculous? Titus still declared that he meant to manage the family brewery. After all his success at Oxford and his popularity, could anything be more absurd than to bury himself in Somerset?

His own name was the first thing that Titus heard as he entered the drawing-room. He greeted it with an approving smile, and sat down by Laura, carefully crossing his long legs.

'She spurns at the brewery, and wants me to take a studio in Hampstead and model bustos,' he explained.

Titus had a soft voice. His speech was gentle and sedate. He chose his words with extreme care, but escaped the charge of affectation by pronouncing them in a hesitating manner.

'I'm sure sculpture is his métier,' said Sibyl. 'Or perhaps poetry. Anyhow, not brewing. I wish you could have seen that little model he made of the grocer at Arcachon.'

Marion said: 'I thought bustos always had wigs.'

'My dear, you've hit it. In fact, that is my objection to this plan for making me a sculptor. Revive the wig, and I object no more. The head is the noblest part of man's anatomy. Therefore enlarge it with a wig.'

Henry thought the conversation was taking a foolish turn. But as host it was his duty to take part in it.

'What about the Elgin Marbles?' he inquired. No wigs there.'

The Peruke and its Functions in Attic Drama, thought Titus, would be a pretty fancy But it would not do for his uncle. Agreeably he admitted that there were no wigs in the Elgin Marbles.

They fell into silence. At an ordinary dinner party Caroline would have felt this silence to be a token that the dinner party was a failure. But this was a family affair, there was no disgrace in having nothing to say. They were all Willoweses and the silence was a seemly Willowes silence. She coula even emphasise it by counting her stitches aloud.

All the chairs and sofas were comfortable. The fire burnt brightly, the curtains hung in solemn folds; they looked almost as solemn as organ pipes. Lolly had gone off into one of her day dreams, just her way, she would never trouble to give a party the least prod. Only Sibyl fidgeted, twisting her heel about in her satin slipper.

'What pretty buckles, Sibyl! Have I seen them before?'

Sibyl had bought them second-hand for next to nothing. They came from Arles, and the old lady who had sold them to her had been such a character. She repeated the characteristic remarks of the old lady in a very competent French accent. Her feet were as slim as ever, and she could stretch them out very prettily. Even in doing so she remembered to ask Caroline where they were going for the Easter holidays.

'Oh, to Blythe, I expect,' said Caroline. 'We know it.'

'When I have evicted my tenants and brewed a large butt of family ale, I shall invite you all down to Lady Place,' said Titus.

'But before then,' said Laura, speaking rather fast, 'I hope you will all come to visit me at Great Mop.'

Every one turned to stare at her in bewilderment.

'Of course, it won't be as comfortable as Lady Place. And I don't suppose there will be room for more than one of you at a time. But I'm sure you'll think it delightful.'

'I don't understand,' said Caroline. 'What is this place, Lolly?'

'Great Mop. It's not really Great. It's in the Chilterns.'

'But why should we go there?'

'To visit me. I'm going to live there.'

'Live there? My dear Lolly!'

'Live there, Aunt Lolly?'

'This is very sudden. Is there really a place called...?'

'Lolly, you are mystifying us.'

They all spoke at once, but Henry spoke loudest, so Laura replied to him.

'No, Henry, I'm not mystifying you. Great Mop is a village in the Chilterns, and I am going to live there, and perhaps keep a donkey. And you must all come on visits.'

'I've never even heard of the place!' said Henry conclusively. 'But you'll love it. "A secluded hamlet in the heart of the Chilterns, Great Mop is situated twelve miles from Wickendon in a hilly district with many beech-woods. The parish church has a fine Norman tower and a squint. The population is 227." And quite close by on a hill there is a ruined windmill, and the nearest railway station is twelve miles off, and there is a farm called Scramble Through the Hedge...'

Henry thought it time to interrupt. 'I suppose you don't expect us to believe all this.'

'I know. It does seem almost too good to be true. But it is. I've read it in a guidebook, and seen it on a map.'

'Well, all I can say is…'

'Henry! Henry!' said Caroline warningly. Henry did not say it. He threw the cushion out of his chair, glared at Laura, and turned away his head.

For some time Titus's attempts at speech had hovered above the tumult, like one holy appeasing dove loosed after the other. The last dove was luckier. It settled on Laura.

'How nice of you to have a donkey. Will it be a grey donkey, like Madam?'

'Do you remember dear Madam, then?'

'Of course I remember dear Madam. I can remember everything that happened to me when I was four. I rode in one pannier, and you, Marion, rode in the other. And we went to have tea in Potts's Dingle.'

'With sponge cakes and raspberry jam, do you remember?'

'Yes. And milk surging in a whisky bottle. Will you have thatch or slate, Aunt Lolly? Slate is very practical.'

'Thatch is more motherly. Anyhow, I shall have a pump.'

'Will it be an indoor or an outdoor pump? I ask, for I hope to pump on it quite often.'

'You will come to stay with me, won't you, Titus?'

Laura was a little cast-down. It did not look, just then, as if anyone else wanted to come and stay with her at Great Mop. But Titus was as sympathetic as she had hoped. They spent the rest of the evening telling each other how she would live. By half-past ten their conjectures had become so fantastic that the rest of the family thought the whole scheme was nothing more than one of Lolly's odd jokes that nobody was ever amused by. Henry took heart. He rallied Laura, supposing that when she lived at Great Mop she would start hunting for catnip again, and become the village witch.

'How lovely!' said Laura.

Henry was satisfied. Obviously Laura could not be in earnest.

When the guests had gone, and Henry had bolted and chained the door, and put out the hall light, Laura hung about a little, thinking that he or Caroline might wish to ask her more. But they asked nothing and went upstairs to bed. Soon after, Laura followed them. As she passed their bedroom door she heard their voices within, the comfortable fragmentary talk of a husband and wife with complete confidence in each other and nothing particular to say.

Laura decided to tackle Henry on the morrow. She observed him during breakfast and saw with satisfaction that he seemed to be in a particularly benign mood. He had drunk three cups of coffee, and said 'Ah! poor fellow!' when a wandering cornet-player began to play on the pavement opposite. Laura took heart from these good omens, and, breakfast being over, and her brother and the Times retired to the study, she followed them thither.

'Henry,' she said. 'I have come for a talk with you.'

Henry looked up. 'Talk away, Lolly,' he said, and smiled at her.

'A business talk,' she continued.

Henry folded the Times and laid it aside. He also (if the expression may be allowed) folded and laid aside his smile.

'Now, Lolly, what is it?'

His voice was kind, but business-like. Laura took a deep breath, twisted the garnet ring round her little finger, and began.

'It has just occurred to me, Henry, that I am forty-seven.'

She paused.

'Go on!' said Henry.

'And that both the girls are married. I don't mean that that has just occurred to me too, but it's part of it. You know, really I'm not much use to you now.'

'My dear Lolly!' remonstrated her brother 'You are extremely useful. Besides, I have never considered our relationship in that light.'

'So I have been thinking. And I have decided that I should like to go and live at Great Mop. You know, that place I was talking about last night.'

Henry was silent. His face was completely blank. Should she recall Great Mop to him by once more repeating the description out of the guide-book?

'In the Chilterns,' she murmured. 'Pop. 227.'

Henry's silence was unnerving her.

'Really, I think it would be a good plan. I should like to live alone in the country. And in my heart I think I have always meant to, one day. But one day is so like another, it's almost impossible to throw salt on its tail. If I don't go soon, I never shall. So if you don't mind, I should like to start as soon as possible.'

There was another long pause. She could not make out Henry at all. It was not like him to say nothing when he was annoyed. She had expected thunders and tramplings, and those she could have weathered. But thus becalmed under a lowering sky she was beginning to lose her head.

At last he spoke.

'I hardly know what to say.'

'I'm sorry if the idea annoys you, Henry.'

'I am not annoyed. I am grieved. Grieved and astonished. For twenty years you have lived under my roof. I have always thought – I may be wrong, but I have always thought – that you were happy here.'

'Quite happy,' said Laura.

'Caroline and I have done all we could to make you so. The children – all the children – look on you as a second mother. We are all devoted to you. And now, without a word of warning, you propose to leave us and go and live at a place called Great Mop. Lolly! I must ask you to put this ridiculous idea out of your head.'

'I never expected you to be so upset, Henry. Perhaps I should have told you more gradually. I should be sorry to hurt you.'

'You have hurt me, I admit,' said he, firmly seizing on this advantage. 'Still, let that pass. Say you won't leave us, Lolly.'

'I'm afraid I can't quite do that.'

'But Lolly, what you want is absurd.'

'It's only my own way, Henry.'

'If you would like a change, take one by all means. Go away for a fortnight. Go away for a month! Take a little trip abroad if you like. But come back to us at the end of it.'

'No, Henry. I love you all, but I feel 1 have lived here long enough.'

'But why? But why? What has come over you I'

Laura shook her head.

'Surely you must have some reasons.'

'I have told you my reasons.'

'Lolly! I cannot allow this. You are my sister. I consider you my charge. I must ask you, once for all to drop this idea. It is not sensible. Or suitable.'

'I have reminded you that I am forty-seven. If I am not old enough now to know what is sensible and suitable, I never shall be.'

'Apparently not.'

This was more like Henry's old form. But though he had scored her off, it did not seem to have encouraged him as much as scoring off generally did He began again, almost as a suppliant.

'Be guided by me, Lolly. At least, take a few days to think it over.'

'No, Henry. I don't feel inclined to; I'd much rather get it over now. Besides, if you are going to disapprove as violently as this, the sooner I pack up and start the better?

'You are mad. You talk of packing up and starting when you have never even set eyes on the place?

'I was thinking of going there to-day, to make arrangements?

'Well, then, you will do nothing of the kind. I'm sorry to see harsh, Lolly. But you must put all this out of your mind?

'Why?'

'It is impracticable'

'Nothing is impracticable for a single, middle-aged woman with an income of her own? Henry paled slightly, and said: 'Your income is no longer what it was?

'Oh, taxes!' said Laura contemptuously. 'Never mind -, even if it's a little less, I can get along on it?

'You know nothing of business, Lolly. I need not enter into explanations with you. It should be enough for me to say that for the last year your income has been practically nonexistent?

'But I can still cash cheques.'

'I have placed a sum at the bank to your credit.'

Laura had grown rather pale too. Her eyes shone.

'I'm afraid you must enter into explanations with me, Henry. After all, it is my income, and I have a right to know what has happened to it.'

'Your capital has always been in my hands, Lolly, and I have administered it as I thought fit.'

'Go on,' said Laura.

'In 1920 I transferred the greater part of it to the Ethiopian Development Syndicate, a perfectly sound investment which will in time be as good as ever, if not better. Unfortunately, owing to this Government and all this socialistic talk the soundest investments have been badly hit. The Ethiopian Development Syndicate is one of them.'

'Go on, Henry. I have understood quite well so far. You have administered all my money into something that doesn't pay. Now explain why you did this.'

'I had every reason for thinking that I should be able to sell out at a profit almost immediately. During November the shares had gone up from 5¾ to 8½. I bought in December at 8½. They went to 8¾ and since then have steadily sunk. They now stand at 4. Of course, my dear, you needn't be alarmed. They will rise again the moment we have a Conservative Government, and that, thank Heaven, must come soon. But you see at present it is out of the question for you to think of leaving us.'

'But don't these Ethiopians have dividends?'

'These,' said Henry with dignity, 'are not the kind of shares that pay dividends. They are – that is to say, they were, and of course will be again – a sound speculative investment. But at present they pay no dividends worth mentioning. Now, Lolly, don't become agitated. I assure you that it is all perfectly all right. But you must give up this idea of the country. Anyhow, I'm sure you wouldn't find it suit you. You are rheumatic—'

Laura tried to interpose.

'—or will be. All the Willoweses are rheumatic. Buckinghamshire is damp. Those poetical beech-woods make it so. You see, trees draw rain. It is one of the principles of afforestation. The trees – that is to say, the rain—'

Laura stamped her foot with impatience. 'Have done with your trumpery red herrings!' she cried.

She had never lost her temper like this before. It was a glorious sensation.

'Henry!' She could feel her voice crackle round his ears. 'You say you bought those shares at eight and something, and that they are now four. So if you sell out now you will get rather less than half what you gave for them.'

'Yes,' said Henry. Surely if Lolly were business woman enough to grasp that so clearly, she would in time see reason on other matters.

'Very well. You will sell them immediately—'

'Lolly!'

'—and reinvest the money in something quite unspeculative and unsound, like War Loan, that will pay a proper dividend I shall still have enough to manage on. I shan't be as comfortable as I thought I should be I shan't be able to afford the little house that I hoped for, nor the donkey But I shan't mind much. It will matter very little to me when I'm there.'

She stopped. She had forgotten Henry, and the unpleasant things she meant to say to him. She had come to the edge of the wood, and felt its cool breath in her face. It did not matter about the donkey, nor the house, nor the darkening orchard even. If she were not to pick fruit from ner own trees, there were common herbs and berries in plenty for her, growing wherever she chose to wander. It is best as one grows older to strip oneself of possessions, to shed oneself downward like a tree, to be almost wholly earth before one dies.

As she left the room she turned and looked at Henry. Such was her mood, she could have blessed him solemnly, as before an eternal departure. But he was sitting with his back to her, and did not look round. When she had gone he took out his handkerchief and wiped his forehead.

Ten days later Laura arrived at Great Mop. After the interview with Henry she encountered no more opposition. Caroline knew better than to persist against an obstinacy which had worsted her husband, and the other members of the family, their surprise being evaporated, were indifferent. Titus was a little taken aback when he found that his aunt's romantic proposals were seriously intended. He for his part was going to Corsica. 'A banal mountainous spot,' he said politely, 'compared with Buckinghamshire.'

The day of Laura's arrival was wet and blusterous. She drove in a car from Wickendon. The car lurched and rattled, and the wind slapped the rain against the windows; Laura could scarcely see the rising undulations of the landscape. When the car drew up before her new home, she stood for a moment looking up the village street, but the prospect was intercepted by the umbrella under which Mrs. Leak hastened to conduct her to the porch. So had it rained and so had the windblown, on the day when she had come on her visit of inspection and had taken rooms in Mrs. Leak's cottage. So, Henry and Caroline and their friends had assured her, did it rain and blow all through the winter in the Chilterns. No words of theirs, they said, could describe how dismal and bleak it would be among those unsheltered hills. To Laura, sitting by the fire in her parlour, the sound of wind and rain was pleasant. 'Weather like this,' she thought, 'would never be allowed in London.'

The unchastened gusts that banged against the side of the house and drove the smoke down the chimney, and the riotous gurgling of the rain in the gutters were congenial to her spirit. 'Hoo! You daredevil,' said the wind. 'Have you come out to join us?' Yet sitting there with no companionship except those exciting voices she was quiet and happy.

Mrs. Leak's tea was strong Indian tea. The bread-and-butter was cut in thick slices, and underneath it was a crocheted mat; there was plum jam in a heart-shaped glass dish, and a plate of rather heavy jam-puffs. It was not quite so good as the farmhouse teas she remembered in Somerset, but a great deal better than teas at Apsley Terrace.

Tea being done with, Laura took stock of her new domain. The parlour was furnished with a large mahogany table, four horsehair chairs and a horsehair sofa, an armchair, and a sideboard, rather girncrack compared to the rest of the furniture. On the walls, which were painted green, hung a print of the Empress Josephine and two rather scowling classical landscapes with ruined temples, and volcanoes. On either side of the hearth were cupboards, and the fireplace was of a cottage pattern with hobs, and a small oven on one side. This fireplace had caught Laura's fancy when she first looked at the rooms. She had stipulated with Mrs. Leak that, should she so wish, she might cook on it. There are some things – mushrooms, for instance, or toasted cheese – which can only be satisfactorily cooked by the eater. Mrs. Leak had made no difficulties. She was an oldish woman, sparing of her words and moderate in her demands. Her husband worked at the sawmill. They were childless. She had never let lodgings before, but till last year an aunt with means of her own had occupied the parlour and bedroom which were now Laura's.

It did not take Laura very long to arrange her belongings, for she had brought little. Soon after supper, which consisted of rabbit, bread and cheese, and table beer, she went upstairs to bed. Moving about her small cold bedroom she suddenly noticed that the wind had fallen, and that it was no longer raining. She pushed aside a corner of the blind and opened the window. The night air was cold and sweet, and the full moon shone high overhead. The sky was cloudless, lovely, and serene; a few stars glistened there like drops of water about to fall For the first time she was looking at the intricate landscape of rounded hills and scooped valleys which she had chosen for learning by heart.

Dark and compact, the beech-woods lay upon the hills. Alighting as noiselessly as an owl, a white cat sprang up on to the garden fence. It glanced from side to side, ran for a yard or two along the top of the fence and jumped off again, going secretly on its way. Laura sighed for happiness. She had no thoughts; her mind was swept as clean and empty as the heavens. For a long time she continued to lean out of the window, forgetting where she was and how she had come there, so unearthly was her contentment.

Nevertheless her first days at Great Mop gave her little real pleasure. She wrecked them by her excitement. Every morning immediately after breakfast she set out to explore the country She believed that by eating a large breakfast she could do without lunch. The days were short, and she wanted to make the most of them, and making the most of the days and going back for lunch did not seem to her to be compatible. Unfortunately, she was not used to making large breakfasts, so her enthusiasm was qualified by indigestion until about four p.m., when both enthusiasm and indigestion yielded to a faintish feeling. Then she turned back, generally by road, since it was growing too dark to find out footpaths, and arrived home with a limp between six and seven. She knew in her heart that she was not really enjoying this sort of thing, but the habit of useless activity was too strong to be snapped by change of scene. And in the evening, as she looked at the map and marked where she had been with little bleeding footsteps of red ink, she was enchanted afresh by the names and the bridle-paths, and, forgetting the blistered heel and the dissatisfaction of that day's walk, planned a new walk for the morrow.

Nearly a week had gone by before she righted herself. She had made an appointment with the sunset that she should see it from the top of a certain hill. The hill was steep, and the road turned and twisted about its sides. It was clear that the sunset would be at their meetingplace before she was, nor would it be likely to kick its heels and wait about for her. She looked at the sky and walked faster. The road took a new and unsuspected turn, concealed behind the clump of trees by which she had been measuring her progress up the hill. She was growing more and more flustered, and at this prick she lost her temper entirely. She was tired, she was miles from Great Mop, and she had made a fool of herself. An abrupt beam of light shot up from behind the hedge as though the sun in vanishing below the horizon had winked at her. 'This sort of thing,' she said aloud, 'has got to be put a stop to.' She sat down in the extremely comfortable ditch to think.

The shades that had dogged her steps up the hill dosed in upon her as she sat in the ditch, but when she took out her map there was enough light to enable her to see where the nearest inn lay. It was close at hand; when she got there she could just read its name on the sign. Its name was The Reason Why. Entering The Reason Why, she ordered tea and a conveyance to drive her back to Great Mop. When she left the inn it was a brilliant night of stars. Outside stood a wagonette drawn by a large white horse. Piled on the seat of the wagonette were a number of waterproof rugs with fingerrings on them, and these she wrapped round her with elaborate care.

The drive back to Great Mop was more filled with glory than anything she had ever experienced. The wagonette creaked over bare hilltops and plunged downwards into the chequered darknesses of unknown winter woods. All the stars shook their glittering spears overhead. Turning this way and that to look at them, the frost pinched her cheeks.

That evening she asked Mrs. Leak if she would lend her some books. From Mrs. Leak's library she chose Mehalah, by the Rev. Sabine Baring-Gould, and an anonymous work of information called Enquire within Upon Everything. The next morning was fine and sunny. She spent it by the parlour fire, reading.

When she read bits of Mehalah she thought how romantic it would be to live in the Essex Marshes. From Enquire Within Upon Everything she learned how gentlemen's hats if plunged in a bath of logwood will come out with a dash of respectability, and that ruins are best constructed of cork. During the afternoon she learned other valuable facts like these, and fell asleep. On the following morning she fell asleep again, in a beechwood, curled up in a heap of dead leaves. After that she had no more trouble. Life becomes simple if one does nothing about it. Laura did nothing about anything for days and days till Mrs. Leak said: 'We shall soon be having Christmas, miss.'

Christmas! So it had caught them all again. By now the provident Caroline herself was suffering the eleventh hour in Oxford Street. But here even Christmas was made easy.

Laura spent a happy afternoon choosing presents at the village shop. For Henry she bought a bottle of ginger wine, a pair of leather gaiters, and some highly recommended tincture of sassafras for his winter cough. For Caroline she bought an extensive parcel – all the shop had, in fact – of variously coloured rug-wools, and a pound's worth of assorted stamps. For Sibyl she bought some tinned fruits, some sugar-biscuits, and a pink knitted bed-jacket. For Fancy and Marion respectively she bought a Swanee flute and a box with Ely Cathedral on the lid, containing string, which Mrs. Trumpet was very glad to see the last of, as it had been forced upon her by a traveller, and had not hit the taste of the village. To her great-nephew and great-nieces she sent postal orders for one guinea, and pink gauze stockings filled with tin toys. These she knew would please, for she had always wanted one herself. For Dunlop she bought a useful button-hook. Acquaintances and minor relations were greeted with picture postcards, either photographs of the local War Memorial Hall and Institute, or a coloured view of some sweet-peas with the motto: 'Kind Thoughts from Great Mop.' A postcard of the latter kind was also enclosed with each of the presents.

Titus was rather more difficult to suit. But by good luck she noticed two heavy glass jars such as old-fashioned druggists use. These were not amongst Mrs. Trumpet's wares – she kept linen buttons in the one and horn buttons in the other; but she was anxious to oblige such a magnificent customer and quite ready to sell her anything that she wanted. She was about to empty out the buttons when Laura stopped her. 'You must keep some for your customers, Mrs. Trumpet. They may want to put them in their Christmas puddings.' Laura was losing her head a little with the excitement. 'But I should like to send about three dozen of each sort, if you can spare them. Buttons are always useful.'

'Yes, miss. Shall I put in some linen thread too?'

Mrs. Trumpet was a stout, obliging woman. She promised to do up all the parcels in thick brown paper and send them off three days before Christmas. As Laura stepped out of the shop in triumph, she exclaimed: 'Well, that's done it!'For the life of her she could not have said in what sense the words were intended. She was divided between admiration for her useful and well-chosen gifts and delight in affronting a kind of good taste which she believed to be merely self-esteem.

Although she had chosen presents with such care for her relations, Laura was surprised when counter presents arrived from them. She had not thought of them as remembering her. Their presents were all of a warm nature; they insisted upon that bleakness and draughtiness which their senders had foretold. When Caroline wrote to thank Laura, she said:

'I have started to make you a nice warm coverlet out of those pretty wools you sent. I think it will look very cheerful and variegated. I often feel quite worried to think of you upon those wind-swept hills. And from all I hear you have a great many woods round you, and I'm afraid all the decaying leaves must make the place damp.'

Heaping coals of fire was a religious occupation. Laura rather admired Caroline for the neat turn of the wrist with which she heaped these.

In spite of the general determination of her family that she should feel the cold Laura lived at Great Mop very comfortably. Mrs. Leak was an excellent cook; she attended to her lodger civilly and kindly enough, made no comments, and showed no curiosity. At times Laura felt as though she had exchanged one Caroline for another. Mrs. Leak was not, apparently, a religious woman. There were no texts on her walls, and when Laura asked for the loan of a Bible Mrs. Leak took a little time to produce it, and blew on the cover before she handed it over. But like Caroline, she gave the impression that her kingdom was not of this world. Laura liked her, and would have been glad to be upon less distant terms with her, but she did not find it easy to break through Mrs. Leak's reserve. She tried this subject and that, but Mrs. Leak did not begin to thaw until Laura said something about black-currant tea. It seemed that Mrs. Leak shared Laura's liking for distillations. That evening she remarked that the table-beer was of her own brewing, and lingered a while with the folded cloth in her hand to explain the recipe. After that Laura was given every evening a glass of home-made wine: dandelion, cowslip, elderberry, ashkey, or mangold. By her appreciation and her inquiries she entrapped Mrs. Leak into pausing longer and longer before she carried away the supper-tray. Before January was out it had become an established thing that after placing the bedroom candlestick on the cleared table Mrs. Leak would sit down and talk for half an hour or so.

There was an indoor pleasantness about these times. Through the wall came the sound of Mr. Leak snoring in the kitchen. The two women sat by the fire, tilting their glasses and drinking in small peaceful sips. The lamplight shone upon the tidy room and the polished table, lighting topaz in the dandelion wine, spilling pools of crimson through the flanks of the bottle of plum gin. It shone on the contented drinkers, and threw their large, close-at-hand shadows upon the wall. When Mrs. Leak smoothed her apron the shadow solemnificd the gesture as though she were moulding an universe. Laura's nose and chin were defined as sharply as the peaks on a holly leaf.

Mrs. Leak did most of the talking. She talked well. She knew a great deal about everybody, and she was not content to quit a character until she had brought it to life for her listener

Mrs. Leak's favourite subject was the Misses Larpent, Miss Minnie and Miss Jane. Miss Minnie was seventy-three, Miss Jane four years younger. Neither of them had known a day's illness, nor any bodily infirmity, nor any relenting of their faculties. They would live for many years yet, if only to thwart their debauched middle-aged nephew, the heir to the estate. Perhaps Miss Willowes had seen Lazzard Court on one of her walks? Yes, Laura had seen it, looking down from a hill-top – the park where sheep were penned among the grouped chestnut trees, the long white house with its expressionless façade – and had heard the stable-clock striking a deserted noon.

The drive of Lazzard Court was five miles long from end to end. The house had fourteen principal bedrooms and a suite for Royalty. Mrs. Leak had been in service at Lazzard Court before her marriage; she knew the house inside and out, and described it to Laura till Laura felt that there was not one of the fourteen principal bedrooms which she did not know. The blue room, the yellow room, the Chinese room, the buff room, the balcony room, the needle-work room – she had slept in them all. Nay, she had awakened in the Royal bed, and pulling aside the red damask curtains had looked to the window to see the sun shining upon the tulip tree.

No visitors slept in the stately bedrooms now, Lazzard Court was very quiet. People in the villages, said Mrs. Leak coldly, called Miss Minnie and Miss Jane two old screws. Mrs. Leak knew better. The old ladies spent lordily upon their pleasures, and economised elsewhere that they might be able to do so. When they invited the Bishop to lunch and gave him stewed rabbit, blackberry pudding, and the best peaches and Madeira that his Lordship was likely to taste in his life, he fared no worse and no better than they fared themselves. Lazzard Court was famous for its racing-stable. To the upkeep of this all meaner luxuries were sacrificed – suitable bonnets, suitable subscriptions, bedroom fires, salmon and cucumber. But the stableyard was like the forecourt of a temple. Every morning after breakfast Miss Jane would go round the stables and feel the horses' legs, her gnarled old hand with its diamond rings slipping over the satin coat.

Nothing escaped the sisters. The dairy, the laundry, the glasshouses, the poultry-yard, all were scrutinised. If any servant were found lacking he or she was called before Miss Minnie in the Justice Room. Mrs. Leak had never suffered such an interview, but she had seen others come away, white-faced, or weeping with apron thrown over head. Even the coffins were made on the estate. Each sister had chosen her elm and had watched it felled, with sharp words for the woodman when he aimed amiss.

When Mrs. Leak had given the last touches to Miss Minnie and Miss Jane, she made Laura's flesh creep with the story of the doctor who took the new house up on the hill. He had been a famous doctor in London, but when he came to Great Mop no one would have anything to do with him. It was said he came as an interloper, watching for old Dr. Halley to die that he might step into his shoes. He grew more and more morose in his lonely house, soon the villagers said he drank; at last came the morning when he and his wife were found dead He had shot her and then himself, so it appeared, and the verdict at the inquest was of Insanity. The chief witnesses were another London doctor, a great man for the brain, who had advised his friend to lead a peaceful country life; and the maidservant, who had heard ranting talk and cries late one evening, and ran out of the house in terror, banging the door behind her, to spend the night with her mother in the village.

After the doctor, Mrs. Leak called up Mr. Jones the clergyman. Laura had seen his white beard browsing among the tombs. He looked like a blessed goat tethered on hallowed grass. He lived alone with his books of Latin and Hebrew and his tame owl which he tried to persuade to sleep in his bedroom. He had dismissed red-haired Emily, the sexton's niece, for pouring hot water on a mouse. Emily had heated the water with the kindest intentions, but she was dismissed nevertheless. Mrs. Leak made much of this incident, for it was Mr. Jones's only act of authority In all other administrations he was guided by Mr. Gurdon, the clerk.

Mr. Gurdon's beard was red and curly (Laura knew him by sight also). Fiery down covered his cheeks, his eyes were small and truculent, and he lived in a small surprised cottage near the church. Every morning he walked forth to the Rectory to issue his orders for the day – this old woman was to be visited with soup, that young one with wrath; and more manure should be ordered for the Rectory cabbages. For Mr. Gurdon was Mr. Jones's gardener, as well as his clerk.

Mr. Gurdon had even usurped the clergyman's perquisite of quarrelling with the organist. Henry Perry was the organist. He had lost one leg and three fingers in a bus accident, so there was scarcely any other profession he could have taken up. And he had always been fond of playing tunes, for his mother, who was a superior widow, had a piano at Rose Cottage.

Mr. Gurdon said that Henry Perry encouraged the choir boys to laugh at him. After church he used to hide behind a yew tree to pounce out upon any choir boys who desecrated the graves by leaping over them. When he caught them he pinched them. Pinches are silent: they can be made use of in sacred places where smacking would be irreverent. One summer Mr. Gurdon told Mr. Jones to forbid the choir treat. Three days later some of the boys were playing with a tricycle. They allowed it to get out of control, and it began to run downhill. At the bottom of the hill was a sharp turn in the road, and Mr. Gurdon's cottage. The tricycle came faster and faster and crashed through the fence into Mr. Gurdon, who was attending to his lettuces and had his back turned. The boys giggled and ran away. Their mothers did not take the affair so lightly. That evening Mr. Gurdon received a large seed-cake, two dozen fresh eggs, a packet of cigarettes, and other appeasing gifts. Next Sunday Mr. Jones in his kind tenor voice announced that a member of the congregation wished to return thanks for mercies lately received. Mr. Gurdon turned round in his place and glared at the choir boys.

Much as he disliked Henry Perry, Mr. Gurdon had disliked the doctor from London even more. The doctor had come upon him frightening an old woman in a field, and had called him a damned bully and a hypocrite. Mr. Gurdon had cursed him back, and swore to be even with him. The old woman bore her defender no better will. She talked in a surly way about her aunt, who was a gipsy and able to afflict people with lice by just looking at them.

Laura did not hear this story from Mrs. Leak. It was told her some time after by Mrs. Trumpet. Mrs. Trumpet hated Mr. Gurdon, though she was very civil to him when he came into the shop. Few people in the village liked Mr. Gurdon, but he commanded a great deal of politeness. Red and burly and to be feared, the clerk reminded Laura of a red bull belonging to the farmer. In one respect he was unlike the bull: Mr. Gurdon was a very respectable man.

Mrs. Leak also told Laura about Mr. and Mrs. Ward, who kept the Lamb and Flag; about Miss Carloe the dressmaker, who fed a pet hedgehog on bread-and-milk; and about fat Mrs. Garland, who let lodgings in the summer and was always so down at heel and jolly.

Although she knew so much about her neighbours, Mrs. Leak was not a sociable woman. The Misses Larpent, the dead doctor, Mr. Jones, Mr. Gurdon, and Miss Carloe – she called them up and caused them to pass before Laura, but in a dispassionate way, rather like the Witch of Endor calling up old Samuel. Nor was Great Mop a sociable village, at any rate compared with the villages which Laura had known as a girl. Never had she seen so little dropping in, leaning over fences, dawdling at the shop or in the churchyard. Little laughter came from the taproom of the Lamb and Flag. Once or twice she glanced in at the window as she passed by and saw the men within sitting silent and abstracted with their mugs before them. Even the bell-ringers when they had finished their practice broke up with scant adieus, and went silently on their way. She had never met country people like these before. Nor had she ever known a village that kept such late hours. Lights were burning in the cottages till one and two in the morning, and she had been awakened at later hours than those by the sound of passing voices. She could hear quite distinctly, for her window was open and faced upon the village street. She heard Miss Carloe say complainingly: 'It's all very well for you young ones. But my old bones ache so, it's a wonder how I get home!' Then she heard the voice of red-haired Emily say: 'No bones so nimble as old bones, Miss Carloe, when it comes to—' and then a voice unknown to Laura said 'Hush'; and she heard no more, for a cock crew. Another night, sometime after this, she heard someone playing a mouth-organ. The music came from far off, it sounded almost as if it were being played out of doors. She lit a candle and looked at her watch – it was halfpast three. She got out of bed and listened at the window; it was a dark night, and the hills rose up like a screen. The noise of the mouthorgan came wavering and veering on the wind. A drunk man, perhaps? Yet what drunk man would play on so steadily? She lay awake for an hour or more, half puzzled, half lulled by the strange music, that never stopped, that never varied, that seemed to have become part of the air.

Next day she asked Mrs. Leak what this strange music could be. Mrs. Leak said that young Billy Thomas was distracted with toothache. He could not sleep, and played for hours nightly upon his mouth-organ to divert himself from the pain. On Wednesday the toothdrawer would come to Barleighs, and young

Billy Thomas would be put out of his agony. Laura was sorry for the sufferer, but she admired the circumstances. The highest flights of her imagination had not risen to more than a benighted drunk. Young Billy Thomas had a finer invention than she.

After a few months she left off speculating about the villagers. She admitted that there was something about them which she could not fathom, but she was content to remain outside the secret, whatever it was. She had not come to Great Mop to concern herself with the hearts of men. Let her stray up the valleys, and rest in the leafless woods that looked so warm with their core of fallen red leaves, and find out her own secret, if she had one; with autumn it might come back to question her. She wondered. She thought not. She felt that nothing could ever again disturb her peace. Wherever she strayed the hills folded themselves round her like the fingers of a hand.

About this time she did an odd thing. In her wanderings she had found a disused well. It was sunk at the side of a green lane, and grass and bushes had grown up around its low rim, almost to conceal it; the wooden frame was broken and mouldered, ropes and pulleys had long ago been taken away, and the water was sunk far down, only distinguishable as an uncertain reflection of the sky. Here, one evening, she brought her guide-book and her map. Pushing aside the bushes she sat down upon the low rim of the well. It was a still, mild evening towards the end of February, the birds were singing, there was a smell of growth in the air, the light lingered in the fields as though it were glad to linger. Looking into the well she watched the reflected sky grow dimmer; and when she raised her eyes the gathering darkness of the landscape surprised her. The time had come. She took the guide-book and the map and threw them in.

She heard the disturbed water sidling against the walls of the well. She scarcely knew what she had done, but she knew that she had done rightly, whether it was that she had sacrificed to the place, or had cast herself upon its mercies – content henceforth to know no more of it than did its own children.

As she reached the village she saw a group of women standing by the milestone. They were silent and abstracted as usual. When she greeted them they returned her greeting, but they said nothing among themselves. After she had gone by they turned as of one accord and began to walk up the field path towards the wood. They were going to gather fuel, she supposed. To-night their demeanour did not strike her as odd. She felt at one with them, an inhabitant like themselves, and she would gladly have gone with them up towards the wood. If they were different from other people, why shouldn't they be? They saw little of the world. Great Mop stood by itself at the head of the valley, five miles from the main road, and cut off by the hills from the other villages. It had a name for being different from other places. The man who had driven Laura home from The Reason Why had said: 'It's not often that a wagonette is seen at Great Mop. It's an out-of-the-way place, if ever there was one. There's no such another village in Buckinghamshire for out-of-the-way-ness. Well may it be called Great Mop, for there's never a Little Mop that I've heard of.'

People so secluded as the inhabitants of Great Mop would naturally be rather silent, and keep themselves close. So Laura thought, and Mr. Saunter was of the same opinion.

Mr. Saunter's words had weight, for he spoke seldom. He was a serious, brown young man, who after the war had refused to go back to his bank in Birmingham. He lived in a wooden hut which he had put up with his own hands, and kept a poultry-farm.

Laura first met Mr. Saunter when she was out walking, early one darkish, wet, January morning. The lane was muddy; she picked her way, her eyes to the ground. She did not notice Mr. Saunter until she was quite close to him. He was standing bareheaded in the rain. His look was sad and gentle, it reflected the mood of the weather, and several dead white hens dangled from his hands. Laura exclaimed, softly, apologetically. This young man was so perfectly of a piece with his surroundings that she felt herself to be an intruder. She was about to turn back when his glance moved slowly towards her. 'Badger,' he said; and smiled in an explanatory fashion Laura knew at once that he had been careless and had left the henhouse door unfastened. She took pains that no shade of blame should mix itself with her condolences. She did not even blame the badger. She knew that this was a moment for nothing but kind words, and not too many of them.

Mr. Saunter was grateful He invited her to come and see his birds. Side by side they turned in silence through a field gate and walked into Mr. Saunter's field. Bright birds were on the sodden grass. As he went by they hurried into their pens, expecting to be fed. 'If you would care to come in,' said Mr. Saunter, 'I should like to make you a cup of tea.'

Mr. Saunter's living-room was very untidy and homelike. A basket of stockings lay on the table. Laura wondered if she might offer to help Mr. Saunter with his mending. But after he had made the tea, he took up a stocking and began to darn it. He darned much better than she did.

As she went home again she fell to wondering what animal Mr. Saunter resembled. But in the end she decided that he resembled no animal except man. Till now, Laura had rejected the saying that man is the noblest work of nature. Half an hour with Mr. Saunter showed her that the saying was true. So had Adam been the noblest work of nature, when he walked out among the beasts, sole overseer of the garden, intact, with all his ribs about him, his equilibrium as yet untroubled by Eve. She had misunderstood the saying merely because she had not happened to meet a man before. Perhaps, like other noble works, man is rare. Perhaps there is only one of him at a time: first Adam; now Mr. Saunter. If that were the case, she was lucky to have met him. This also was the result of coming to Great Mop.

So much did Mr. Saunter remind Laura of Adam that he made her feel like Eve – for she was petitioned by an unlady-like curiosity. She asked Mrs. Leak about him. Mrs. Leak could tell her nothing that was not already known to her, except that young Billy Thomas went up there every day on his bicycle to lend Mr. Saunter a hand. Laura would not stoop to question young Billy Thomas. She fought againsl her curiosity, and the spring came to her aid.

This new year was changing her whole com ception of spring. She had thought of it as a denial of winter, a green spear that thrust through a tyrant's rusty armour. Now she saw it as something filial, gently unlacing the helm of the old warrior and comforting his rough cheek. In February came a spell of fine weather. She spent whole days sitting in the woods, where the wood-pigeons moaned for pleasure on the boughs. Sometimes two cock birds would tumble together in mid air, shrieking, and buffeting with their wings, and then would fly back to the quivering boughs and nurse the air into peace again. All round her the sap was rising up. She laid her cheek against a tree and shut her eyes to listen. She expected to hear the tree drumming like a telegraph pole.

It was so warm in the woods that she forgot that she sat there for shelter. But though the wind blew lightly, it blew from the east. In March the wind went round to the south-west. It brought rain. The bright, cold fields were dimmed and warm to walk in now. Like embers the wet beech-leaves smouldered in the woods.

All one day the wind had risen, and late in the evening it called her out. She went up to the top of Cubbey Ridge, past the ruined windmill that clattered with its torn sails. When she had come to the top of the Ridge she stopped, with difficulty holding herself upright. She felt the wind swoop down close to the earth. The moon was out hunting overhead, her pack of black and white hounds ranged over the sky. Moon and wind and clouds hunted an invisible quarry. The wind routed through the woodi Laura from the hill-top heard the various surrounding woods cry out with different voices. The spent gusts left the beech-hangers throbbing like sea caverns through which the wave had passed, the fir plantation seemed to chant some never-ending rune.

Listening to these voices, another voice came to her ear – the far-off pulsation of a goods train labouring up a steep cutting. It was scarcely audible, more perceptible as feeling than as sound, but by its regularity it dominated all the other voices. It seemed to come nearer and nearer, to inform her like the drumming of blood in her ears. She began to feel defenceless, exposed to the possibility of an overwhelming terror. She listened intently, trying not to think. Though the noise came from an ordinary goods train, no amount of reasoning could stave off this terror.

She must yield herself, yield up all her attention, if she would escape. It was a wicked sound. It expressed something eternally outcast and reprobated by man, stealthily trafficking by night, unseen in the dark clefts of the hills. Loud, separate, and abrupt, each pant of the engine trampled down her wits. The wind and the moon and the ranging cloud pack were not the only hunters abroad that night: something else was hunting among the hills, hunting slowly, deliberately, sure of its quarry.

Suddenly she remembered the goods yard at Paddington, and all her thoughts slid together again like a pack of hounds that have picked up the scent They streamed faster and faster; she clenched her hands and prayed as when a child she had prayed in the hunting-field.

In the goods yard at Paddington she had almost pounced on the clue, the clue to the secret country of her mind. The country was desolate and half-lit, and she walked there alone, mistress of it, and mistress, too, of the terror that roamed over the blank fields and haunted round her. Here was country just so desolate and half-lit. She was alone, just as in her dreams, and the terror had come to keep her company, and crouched by her side, half in fawning, half in readiness to pounce. All this because of a goods train that laboured up a cutting. What was this cabal of darkness, suborning her own imagination to plot against her? What were these iron hunters doing near mournful, ever-weeping Paddington?

'Now! Now!' said the moon, and plunged towards her through the clouds.

Baffled, she stared back at the moon and shook her head. For a moment it had seemed as though the clue were found, but it had slid through her hands again. The train had reached the top of the cutting, with a shriek of delight it began to pour itself downhill. She smiled. It amused her to suppose it loaded with cabbages. Arrived at Paddington, the cabbages would be diverted to Covent Garden. But inevitably, and with all the augustness of due course, they would reach their bourne at Apsley Terrace. They would shed all their midnight devilry in the pot, and be served up to Henry and Caroline very pure and vegetable.

'Lovely! lovely!' she said, and began to descend the hill, for the night was cold. Though her secret had eluded her again, she did nol mind. She knew that this time she had come nearer to catching it than ever before. If it were attainable she would run it to earth here, sooner or later. Great Mop was the likeliest place to find it.

The village was in darkness; it had gone to bed early, as good villages should. Only Miss Carloe's window was alight. Kind Miss Carloe, she would sit up till all hours tempting her hedgehog with bread-and-milk. Hedgehogs are nocturnal animals; they go out for walks at night, grunting, and shoving out their black snouts. 'Thrice the brindled cat hath mewed; Thrice, and once the hedgepig whined. Harper cries, "'Tis time, 'tis time."' She found the key under the half-brick, and let herself in very quietly. Only sleep sat up for her, waiting in the hushed house. Sleep took her by the hand, and convoyed her up the narrow stairs. She fell asleep almost as her head touched the pillow.

By the next day all this seemed very ordinary. She had gone out on a windy night and heard a goods train. There was nothing remarkable in that. It would have been a considerable adventure in London, but it was nothing in the Chilterns. Yet she retained an odd feeling of respect for what had happened, as though it had laid some command upon her that waited to be interpreted and obeyed. She thought it over, and tried to make sense of it. If it pointed to anything, it pointed to Paddington. She did what she could; she wrote and invited Caroline to spend a day at Great Mop. She did not suppose that this was the right interpretation, but she could think of no other.

All the birds were singing as Laura went down the lane to meet Caroline's car. It was almost like summer, nothing could be more fortunate. Caroline was dressed in sensible tweeds. 'It was raining when I left London,' she said, and glanced severely at Laura's cotton gown.

'Was it?' said Laura. 'It hasn't rained here.' She stopped. She looked carefully at the blue sky. There was not a cloud to be seen. 'Perhaps it will rain later on,' she added. Caroline also looked at the sky, and said: 'Probably.'

Conversation was a little difficult, for Laura did not know how much she was still in disgrace. She asked after everybody in a rather guilty voice, and heard how emphatically they all throve, and what a pleasant, cheerful winter they had all spent. After that came the distance from Wickendon and the hour of departure. In planning the conduct of the day, Laura had decided to keep the church for after lunch. Before lunch she would show Caroline the view. She had vaguely allotted an hour and a half to the view, but it took scarcely twenty minutes. At least, that was the time it took walking up to the windmill and down again. The view had taken no time at all. It was a very clear day, and everything that could be seen was perceptible at the first glance.

Caroline was so stoutly equipped for country walking that Laura had not the heart to drag her up another hill. They visited the church instead. The church was more successful.

Caroline sank on her knees and prayed. This gave Laura an opportunity to look round, for she had not been inside the church before. It was extremely narrow, and had windows upon the south side only, so that it looked like a holy corridor. Caroline prayed for some time, and Laura made the most of it. Presently she was able to lead Caroline down the corridor, murmuring: 'That window was presented in 1901. There is rather a nice brass in this corner. That bit of carving is old, it is the Wise and the Foolish Virgins. Take care of the step.'

One foolish Virgin pleased Laura as being particularly life-like. She stood a little apart from the group, holding a flask close to her ear, and shaking it. During lunch Laura felt that her stock of oil, too, was running very low. But it was providentially renewed, for soon after lunch a perfect stranger fell off a bicycle just outside Mrs. Leak's door and sprained her ankle. Laura and Caroline leapt up to succour her, and then there was a great deal of cold compress and hot tea and animation. The perfect stranger was a Secretary to a Guild. She asked Caroline if she did not think Great Mop a delightful nook, and Caroline cordially agreed. They went on discovering Committees in common till tea-time, and soon after went off together in Caroline's car. Just as Caroline stepped into the car she asked Laura if she had met any nice people in the neighbourhood.

'No. There aren't any nice people,' said Laura. Wondering if the bicycle would stay like that, twined so casually round the driver's neck, she had released her attention one minute too soon.

As far as she knew this was her only slip throughout the day. It was a pity. But Caroline would soon forget it; she might not even have heard it, for the Secretary was talking loudly about

Homes of Rest at the same moment. Still, it was a pity. She might have remembered Mr. Saunter, though perhaps she could not have explained him satisfactorily in the time.

She turned and walked slowly through the fields towards the poultry-farm. She could not settle down to complete solitude so soon after Caroline's departure. She would decline gradually, using Mr. Saunter as an intermediate step. He was feeding his poultry, going from pen to pen with a zinc wheelbarrow and a large wooden spoon. The birds flew round him; he had continually to stop and fend them off like a swarm of large midges. Sometimes he would grasp a specially bothering bird and throw it back into the pen as though it were a ball. She leant on the gate and watched him. This young man who had been a bank-clerk and a soldier walked with the easy, slow strides of a born countryman; he seemed to possess the earth with each step. No doubt but he was like Adam. And she, watching him from above – for the field sloped down from the gate to the pens – was like God. Did God, after casting out the rebel angels and before settling down to the peace of a heaven unpeopled of contradiction, use Adam as an intermediate step?

On his way back to the hut Mr. Saunter noticed Laura. He came up and leant on his side of the gate. Though the sun had gone down, the air was still warm, and a disembodied daylight seemed to weigh upon the landscape like a weight of sleep. The birds which had sung all day now sang louder than ever.

'Hasn't it been a glorious day?' said Mr. Saunter.

'I have had my sister-in-law down,' Laura answered. 'She lives in London.'

'My people,' said Mr. Saunter, 'all live in the Midlands.'

'Or in Australia,' he added after a pause.

Mr. Saunter, seen from above, walking among his flocks and herds – for even hens seemed ennobled into something Biblical by their relation to him – was an impressive figure. Mr. Saunter leaning on the gate was a pleasant, unaffected young man enough, but no more. Quitting him, Laura soon forgot him as completely as she had forgotten Caroline. Caroline was a tedious bluebottle; Mr. Saunter a gentle, furry brown moth; but she could brush off one as easily as the other.

Laura even forgot that she had invited the moth to settle again; to come to tea. It was only by chance that she had stayed indoors that afternoon, making currant scones. To amuse herself she had cut the dough into likenesses of the village people. Curious developments took place in the baking. Miss Carloe's hedgehog had swelled until it was almost as large as its mistress. The dough had run into it, leaving a great hole in Miss Carloe's side. Mr. Jones had a lump on his back, as though he were carrying the Black Dog in a bag; and a fancy portrait of Miss Larpent in her elegant youth and a tight-fitting sweeping amazon had warped and twisted until it was more like a gnarled thorn tree than a woman.

Laura felt slightly ashamed of her freak. It was unkind to play these tricks with her neighbours' bodies. But Mr. Saunter ate the strange shapes without comment, quietly splitting open the villagers and buttering them. He told her that he would soon lose the services of young Billy Thomas, who was going to Lazzard Court as a footman.

'I shouldn't think young Billy Thomas would make much of a footman,' said Laura.

'I don't know,' he answered consideringly. 'He's very good at standing still.'

Laura had brought her sensitive conscience into the country with her, just as she had brought her umbrella, though so far she had not remembered to use either. Now the conscience gave signs of life. Mr. Saunter was so nice, and had eaten up those derisive scones, innocently under the impression that they had been prepared for him; he had come with his gift of eggs, all kindness and forethought while she had forgotten his existence; and now he was getting up to go, thanking her and afraid that he had stayed too long. She had acted unworthily by this young man, so dignified and unassuming; she must do something to repair the slight she had put upon him in her own mind. She offered herself as a substitute for young Billy Thomas until Mr. Saunter could find someone else.

'I don't know anything about hens,' she admitted. 'But I am fond of animals, and I am very obedient.'

It was agreed that she might go on the following day to help him with the trap-nesting, and see how she liked it.

At first Mr. Saunter would not allow her to do more than walk round with him upon planks specially put down to save her from the muddy places, pencil the eggs, and drink tea afterwards. But she came so punctually and showed such eagerness that as time went on she persuaded him into allowing her a considerable share in the work.

There was much to do, for it was a busy time of year. The incubators had fulfilled their time; Laura learnt how to lift out the newly-hatched chicks, damp, almost lifeless from their birth-throes, and pack them into baskets. A few hours after the chicks were plump and fluffy. They looked like bunches of primroses in the moss-lined baskets.

Besides mothering his chicks Mr. Saunter was busy with a great re-housing of the older birds. This was carried out after sundown, for the birds were sleepy then, and easier to deal with. If moved by day they soon revolted, and went back to their old pens. Even as it was there were always a few sticklers, roosting uncomfortably among the newcomers, or standing disconsolately before their old homes, closed against them.

Laura liked this evening round best of all. The April twilights were marvellously young and still. A slender moon soared in the green sky; the thick spring grass was heavy with dew, and the earth darkened about her feet while overhead it still seemed quite light. Mr. Saunter would disappear into the henhouse, a protesting squawking and scuffling would be heard; then he would emerge with hens under either arm. He showed Laura how to carry them, two at a time, their breasts in her hands, their wings held fast between her arm and her side. She would tickle the warm breasts, warm and surprisingly bony with quills under the soft plumage, and make soothing noises.

At first she felt nervous with the strange burden, so meek and inanimate one moment, so shrewish the next, struggling and beating with strong freed wings. However many birds Mr. Saunter might be carrying, he was always able to relieve her of hers. Immediately the termagant would subside, tamed by the large sure grasp, meek as a dove, with rigid dangling legs, and head turning sadly from side to side.

Laura never became as clever with the birds as Mr. Saunter. But when she had overcome her nervousness she managed them well enough to give herself a great deal of pleasure. They nestled against her, held fast in the crook of her arm, while her fingers probed among the soft feathers and rigid quills of their breasts.

She liked to feel their acquiescence, their dependence upon her. She felt wise and potent. She remembered the henwife in the fairy-tales, she understood now why kings and queens resorted to the henwife in their difficulties. The henwife held their destinies in the crook of her arm, and hatched the future in her apron. She was sister to the spaewife, and close cousin to the witch, but she practised her art under cover of henwifery; she was not, like her sister and her cousin, a professional. She lived unassumingly at the bottom of the king's garden, wearing a large white apron and very possibly her husband's cloth cap; and when she saw the king and queen coming down the gravel path she curtseyed reverentially, and pretended it was the eggs they had come about. She was easier of approach than the spaewife, who sat on a creepie and stared at the smouldering peats till her eyes were red and unseeing; or the witch, who lived alone in the wood, her cottage window all grown over with brambles. But though she kept up this pretence of homeliness she was not inferior in skill to the professionals. Even the pretence of homeliness was not quite so homely as it might seem. Laura knew that the Russian witches live in small huts mounted upon three giant hen's legs, all yellow and scaly. The legs can go; when the witch desires to move her dwelling the legs stalk through the forest, clattering against the trees, and printing long scars upon the snow.

Following Mr. Saunter up and down between the pens, Laura almost forgot where and who she was, so completely had she merged her personality into the henwife's. She walked back along the rutted track and down the steep lane as obliviously as though she were flitting home on a broomstick. All through April she helped Mr. Saunter. They were both sorry when a new boy applied for the job and her duties came to an end. She knew no more of Mr. Saunter at the close of this association than she had known at its beginning. It could scarcely be said even that she liked him any better, for from their first meeting she had liked him extremely. Time had assured the liking, and that was all. So well assured was it, that she felt perfectly free to wander away and forget him once more, certain of finding him as likeable and well liked as before whenever she might choose to return.

During her first months at Great Mop the moods of the winter landscape and the renewing of spring had taken such hold of her imagination that she thought no season could be more various and lovely. She had even written a slightly precious letter to Titus – for somehow correspondence with Titus was always rather attentive – declaring her belief that the cult of the summer months was a piece of cockney obtuseness, a taste for sweet things, and a preference for dry grass to strew their egg-shells upon. But with the first summer days and the first cowslips she learnt better. She had known that there would be cowslips in May; from the day she first thought of Great Mop she had promised them to herself. She had meant to find them early and watch the yellow blossoms unfolding upon the milky green stems. But they were beforehand with her, or she had watched the wrong fields. When she walked into the meadow it was bloomed over with cowslips, powdering the grass in variable plenty, here scattered, there clustered, innumerable as the stars in the Milky Way.

She knelt down among them and laid her face close to their fragrance. The weight of all her unhappy years seemed for a moment to weigh her bosom down to the earth; she trembled, understanding for the first time how miserable she had been; and in another moment she was released. It was all gone, it could never be again, and never had been. Tears of thankfulness ran down her face. With every breath she drew, the scent of the cowslips flowed in and absolved her.

She was changed, and knew it. She was humbler, and more simple. She ceased to triumph mentally over her tyrants, and rallied herself no longer with the consciousness that she had outraged them by coming to live at Great Mop. The amusement she had drawn from their disapproval was a slavish remnant, a derisive dance on the north bank of the Ohio There was no question of forgiving them. She had not, in any case, a forgiving nature; and the injury they had done her was not done by them. If she were to start forgiving she must needs forgive Society, the Law, the Church, the History of Europe, the Old Testament, greatgreat-aunt Salome and her prayer-book, the Bank of England, Prostitution, the Architect of Apsley Terrace, and half a dozen other useful props of civilisation. All she could do was to go on forgetting them. But now she was able to forget them without flouting them by her forgetfulness.

Throughout May and June and the first fortnight of July she lived in perfect idleness and contentment, growing every day more freckled and more rooted in peace. On July 17th she was disturbed by a breath from the world. Titus came down to see her. It was odd to be called Aunt Lolly again. Titus did not use the term often; he addressed his friends of both sexes and his relations of all ages as My Dear; but Aunt Lolly slipped out now and again.

There was no need to show Titus the inside of the church. There was no need even to take him up to the windmill and show him the view. He did all that for himself, and got it over before breakfast – for Titus breakfasted for three mornings at Great Mop. He had come for the day only, but he was too pleased to go back. He was his own master now, he had rooms in Bloomsbury and did not need even to send off a telegram. Mrs. Garland who let lodgings in the summer was able to oblige him with a bedroom, full of pincushions and earwigs and marine photographs; and Mrs. Trumpet gave him all the benefit of all the experience he invoked in the choice of a tooth-brush. For three days he sat about with Laura, and talked of his intention to begin brewing immediately. He had refused to visit Italy with his mother – he had rejected several flattering invitations from editors – because brewing appealed to him more than anything else in the world. This, he said, was the last night out before the wedding. On his return to Bloomsbury he intended to let his rooms to an amiable Mahometan, and to apprentice himself to his family brewery until he had learnt the family trade.

Laura gave him many messages to Lady Place. It was clear before her in an early morning light. She could exactly recall the smell of the shrubbery, her mother flowing across the croquet lawn, her father's voice as he called up the dogs. She could see herself, too: her old self, for her present self had no part in the place. She did not suppose she would ever return there, although she was glad that Titus was faithful.

Titus departed. He wrote her a letter from Bloomsbury, saying that he had struck a good bargain with the Mahometan, and was off to Somerset. Ten days later she heard from Sibyl that he was coming to live at Great Mop. She had scarcely time to assemble her feelings about this before he was arrived.

PART III

It was the third week in Ausust. The weather was sultry; day after day Laura heard the village people telling each other that there was thunder in the air. Every evening they stood in the village street, looking upwards, and the cattle stood waiting in the fields. But the storm delayed. It hid behind the hills, biding its time.

Laura had spent the afternoon in a field, a field of unusual form, for it was triangular. On two sides it was enclosed by woodland, and because of this it was already darkening into a premature twilight, as though it were a room. She had been there for hours. Though it was sultry, she could not sit still. She walked up and down, turning savagely when she came to the edge of the field. Her limbs were tired, and she stumbled over the flints and matted couch-grass. Throughout the long afternoon a stock-dove had cooed in the wood. 'Cool, cool, cool,' it said, delighting in its green bower. Now it had ceased, and there was no life in the woods. The sky was covered with a thick uniform haze. No ray of the declining sun broke through it, but the whole heavens were beginning to take on a dull, brassy pallor. The long afternoon was ebbing away, stealthily, impassively, as though it were dying under an anaesthetic.

Laura had not listened to the stock-dove; she had not seen the haze thickening overhead. She walked up and down in despair and rebellion. She walked slowly, for she felt the weight of her chains. Once more they had been fastened upon her. She had worn them for many years, acquiescently, scarcely feeling their weight. Now she felt it. And, with their weight, she felt their familiarity, and the familiarity was worst of all. Titus had seen her starting out. He had cried: 'Where are you off to, Aunt Lolly? Wait a minute, and I'll come too.' She had feigned not to hear him and had walked on. She had not turned her head until she was out of the village, she expected at every moment to hear him come bounding up behind her. Had he done so, she thought she would have turned round and snarled at him. For she wanted, oh! how much she wanted, to be left alone for once. Even when she felt pretty sure that she had escaped she could not profit by her solitude, for Titus's voice still jangled on her nerves. 'Where are you off to, Aunt Lolly? Wait a minute, and I'll come too.' She heard his very tones, and heard intensely her own silence that had answered him. Too flustered to notice where she was going, she had followed a chance track until she found herself in this field where she had never been before. Here the track ended, and here she stayed.

The woods rose up before her like barriers. On the third side of the field was a straggling hedge; along it sprawled a thick bank of burdocks, growing with malignant profusion. It was an unpleasant spot. Bitterly she said to herself: 'Well, perhaps he'll leave me alone here,' and was glad of its unpleasantness.

Titus could have all the rest: the green meadows, the hill-tops, the beech-woods dark and resonant as the inside of a sea-shell. He could walk in the greenest meadow and have dominion over it like a bull. He could loll his great body over the hill-tops, or rout silence out of the woods. They were hers, they were all hers, but she would give them all up to him and keep only this dismal field, and these coarse weeds growing out of an uncleansed soil. Any terms to be rid of him. But even on these terms she could not be rid of him, for all the afternoon he had been present in her thoughts, and his voice rang in her ears as distinctly as ever: 'Wait a minute, and I'll come with you.' She had not waited; but, nevertheless, he had come.

Actually, she knew – and the knowledge smote her – Titus, seeing her walk by unheeding, had picked up his book again and read on, reading slowly, and slowly drawing at his pipe, careless, intent, and satisfied. Perhaps he still sat by the open window. Perhaps he had wandered out, taking his book with him, and now was lying in the shade, still reading, or sleeping with his nose pressed into the grass, or with idle patience inveigling an ant to climb up a dry stalk. For this was Titus, Titus who had always been her friend. She had believed that she loved him; even when she heard that he was coming to live at Great Mop she had half thought that it might be rather nice to have him there. 'Dearest Lolly,' Sibyl had written from Italy, 'I feel quite reconciled to this wild scheme of Tito's, since you will be there to keep an eye on him. Men are so helpless. Tito is so impracticable. A regular artist,' etc.

The helpless artist had arrived, and immediately upon his arrival walked out to buy beer and raspberries. Sibyl might feel perfectly reconciled. No cat could jump into the most comfortable armchair more unerringly than Titus. 'Such a nice young gentleman,' said Mrs. Garland, smoothing his pyjamas with a voluptuous hand. 'Such a nice young gentleman,' said Miss Carloe, rubbing her finger over the milling of the new florin she received for the raspberries. 'Such a nice young gentleman,' said Mrs. Trumpet at the shop, and Mrs. Ward at the Lamb and Flag. All the white-aproned laps opened to dandle him. The infant Bacchus walked down the village street with his beer and his raspberries, bowing graciously to all Laura's acquaintances. That evening he supped with her and talked about Fuseli. Fuseli – pronounced Foozley – was a neglected figure of the utmost importance. The pictures, of course, didn't matter: Titus supposed there were some at the Tate. It was Fuseli the man, Fuseli the sign of his times, etc., that Titus was going to write about. It had been the ambition of his life to write a book about Fuseli, and his first visit to Great Mop convinced him that this was the perfect place to write it in. The secret, Titus said, of writing a good book was to be cut off from access to the reading-room of the British Museum. Laura said a little pettishly that if that were all Titus might have stayed in Bloomsbury, and written his book on Good Fridays. Titus demurred. Suppose he ran out of ink? No! Great Mop was the place. 'To-morrow,' he added, 'you must take me round and show me all your footpaths.'

He left his pipe and tobacco pouch on the mantelpiece. They lay there like the orb and sceptre of an usurping monarch. Laura dreamed that night that Fuseli had arrived at Mr. Saunter's poultry-farm, killed the hens, and laid out the field as a golf-course.

She heard a great deal about Fuseli during the next few days, while she was obediently showing Titus all her footpaths. It was hot, so they walked in the woods. The paths were narrow, there was seldom room for two to walk abreast, so Titus generally went in front, projecting his voice into the silence. She disliked these walks; she felt ashamed of his company; she thought the woods saw her with him and drew back scornfully to let them pass by together.

Titus was more tolerable in the village street. Indeed, at first she was rather proud of her nephew's success. After a week he knew everybody, and knew them far better than she did. He passed from the bar-parlour of the Lamb and Flag to the rustic woodwork of the rector's lawn. He subscribed to the bowling-green fund, he joined the cricket club, he engaged himself to give readings at the Institute during the winter evenings. He was invited to become a bell-ringer, and to read the lessons. He burgeoned with projects for Co-operative Blue Beverens, inorris-dancing, performing Coriolanus with the Ancient Foresters, getting Henry Wappenshaw to come down and paint a village sign, inviting Pandora Williams and her rebeck for the Barleighs Flower Show. He congratulated Laura upon having discovered so unspoilt an example of the village community.

After the first fortnight he was less exuberant in the growth of his vast fronds. He was growing downwards instead, rooting into the soil. He began his book, and promised to stand godfather to the roadman's next child. When they went for walks together he would sometimes fall silent, turning his head from side to side to browse the warm scent of a clover field. Once, as they stood on the ridge that guarded the valley from the south-east, he said: 'I should like to stroke it' – and he waved his hand towards the pattern of rounded hills embossed with rounded beech-woods. She felt a cold shiver at his words, and turned away her eyes from the landscape that she loved so jealously. Titus could never have spoken so if he had not loved it too. Love it as he might, with all the deep Willowes love for country sights and smells, love he never so intimately and soberly, his love must be a horror to her. It was different in kind from hers. It was comfortable, it was portable, it was a reasonable appreciative appetite, a possessive and masculine love. It almost estranged her from Great Mop that he should be able to love it so well, and express his love so easily. He loved the countryside as though it were a body.

She had not loved it so. For days at a time she had been unconscious of its outward aspect, for long before she saw it she had loved it and blessed it. With no earnest but a name, a few lines and letters on a map, and a spray of beechleaves, she had trusted the place and staked everything on her trust. She had struggled to come, but there had been no such struggle for Titus. It was as easy for him to quit Bloomsbury for the Chilterns as for a cat to jump from a hard chair to a soft. Now after a little scrabbling and exploration he was curled up in the green lap and purring over the landscape. The green lap was comfortable. He meant to stay in it, for he knew where he was well off. It was so comfortable that he could afford to wax loving, praise its kindly slopes, stretch out a discriminating paw and pat it. But Great Mop was no more to him than any other likeable country lap. He liked it because he was in possession. His comfort apart, it was a place like any other place.

Laura hated him for daring to love it so. She hated him for daring to love it at all. Most of all she hated him fur imposing his kind of love on her. Since he had come to Great Mop she had not been allowed to love in her own way. Commenting, pointing out, appreciating, Titus tweaked her senses one after another as if they ¿verc so many bell-ropes. He was a good judge of country things; little escaped him, he understood the points of a landscape as James his father had understood the points of a horse. This was not her way. She was ashamed at paying the countryside these horse-coping compliments. Day by day the spirit of the place withdrew itself further from her. The woods judged her by her company, and hushed their talk as she passed by with Titus. Silence heard them coming, and fled out of the fields, the hills locked up their thoughts, and became so many grassy mounds to be walked up and walked down. She was being boycotted, and she knew it. Presently she would not know it any more. For her too Great Mop would be a place like any other place, a pastoral landscape where an aunt walked out with her nephew.

Nothing was left her but this sour field. Even this was not truly hers, for here also Titus walked beside her and called her Aunt Lolly. She was powerless against him. He had no idea how he had havocked her peace of mind, he was making her miserable in the best of faith. If he could guess, or if she could tell him, what ruin he carried with him, he would have gone away. She admitted that, even in her frenzy of annoyance. Titus had a kind heart, he meant her nothing but good. Besides, he could easily find another village, other laps were as smooth and as green. But that would never happen. He would never guess. It would never occur to him to look for resentment in her face, or to speculate upon the mood of any one he knew so well. And she would never be able to tell him. When she was with him she came to heel and resumed her old employment of being Aunt Lolly. There was no way out.

In vain she had tried to escape, transient and delusive had been her ecstasies of relief. She had thrown away twenty years of her life like a handful of old rags, but the wind had blown them back again, and dressed her in the old uniform. The wind blew steadily from the old quarter, it was the same east wind that chivied bits of waste paper down Apsley Terrace. And she was the same old Aunt Lolly, so useful and obliging and negligible.

The field was full of complacent witnesses. Titus had let them in. Henry and Caroline and Sibyl, Fancy and Marion and Mr. Wolf-Saunders stood round about her; they recognised her and cried out: 'Why, Aunt Lolly, what are you doing here?' And Dunlop came stealthily up behind her and said: 'Excuse me, Miss Lolly, I thought you might like to know that the warning gong has gone!' She stood at bay, trembling before them, shaken and sick with the grinding anger of the slave. They were come out to recapture her, they had tracked her down and closed her in. They had let her run a little way – that was all – for they knew they could get her back when they chose. Her delusion of freedom had amused them. They had stood grinning behind the bushes when she wept in the cowslip field.

It had been quite entertaining to watch her, for she had taken herself and her freedom so seriously, happy and intent as a child keeping house under the table. They had watched awhile in their condescending grown-up way, and now they approached her to end the game. Henry was ready to overlook her rebellion, his lips glistened with magnanimity; Caroline and Sibyl came smiling up to twine their arms round her waist; the innocent children of Fancy and Marion stretched out their hands to her and called her Aunt Lolly. And Titus, who had let them in, stood a little apart like a showman, and said, 'You see, it's all right. She's just the same.'

They were all leagued against her. They were come out to seize on her soul. They were invulnerably sure of their prey.

'No!' she cried out, wildly clapping her hands together. 'No! You shan't get me. I won't go back. I won't… Oh! Is there no help?'

The sound of her voice frightened her. She heard its desperate echo rouse the impassive wood. She raised her eyes and looked round her. The field was empty. She trembled, and felt cold. The sultry afternoon was over. Dusk and a clammy chill seemed to creep out from among the darkening trees that waited there so stilly. It was as though autumn had come in the place of twilight, and the colourless dark hue of the field dazzled before her eyes. She stood in the middle of the field, waiting for an answer to her cry. There was no answer. And yet the silence that had followed it had been so intent, so deliberate, that it was like a pledge. If any listening power inhabited this place; if any grimly favourable power had been evoked by her cry; then surely a compact had been made, and the pledge irrevocably given.

She walked slowly towards the wood. She was incredibly fatigued; she could scarcely drag one foot after the other Her mind was almost a blank. She had forgotten Titus; she had forgotten the long afternoon of frenzy and bewilderment. Everything was unreal except the silence that followed after her outcry. As she came to the edge of the wood she heard the mutter of heavy foliage. 'No!' the woods seemed to say, 'No! We will not let you go.'

She walked home unheedingly, almost as though she were walking in her sleep. The chance contact with a briar or a tall weed sent drowsy tinglings through her flesh. It was with surprise that she looked down from a hillside and saw the crouched roofs of the village before her.

The cottage was dark, Laura remembered that Mrs. Leak had said that she was going out to a lecture at the Congregational Hall that evening. As she unlocked the door she smiled at the thought of having the house all to herself. The passage was cool and smelt of linoleum. She heard the kitchen clock ticking pompously as if it, too, were pleased to have the house to itself. When Mrs. Leak went out and left the house empty, she was careful to lock the door of Laura's parlour and to put the key under the case with the stuffed owl. Laura slid her fingers into the dark slit between the bottom of the case and the bracket. The key was cold and sleek; she liked the feel of it, and the obliging way it turned in the lock.

As she entered the room, she sniffed. It smelt a little fusty from being shut up on a warm evening. Her nose distinguished Titus's tobacco and the hemp agrimony that she had picked the day before. But there was something else – a faintly animal smell which she could not account for. She threw up the rattling window and turned to light the lamp. Under the green shade the glow whitened and steadied itself. It illuminated the supper-table prepared for her, the shining plates, the cucumber and the radishes, the neat slices of cold veal and the glistening surface of the junket. Nameless and patient, these things had been waiting in the dark, waiting for her to come back and enjoy them. They met her eye with self-possession. They had been sure that she would be pleased to see them. Her spirits shot up, as the flame of the lamp had cleared and steadied itself a moment before. She forgot all possibility of distress. She thought only of the moment, and of the certainty with which she possessed it. In this mood of sleepy exaltation she stood and looked at the supper-table. Long before she had come to Great Mop, the shining plates had come. Four of them, she knew from Mrs. Leak, had been broken; one was too much scorched in the oven to be presentable before her. But these had survived that she might come and eat off them. The quiet cow that had yielded so quietly the milk for her junket had wandered in the fields of Great Mop long before she saw them, or saw them in fancy. The radishes and cucumbers sprang from old and well-established Great Mop families. Her coming had been foreseen, her way had been prepared. Great Mop was infallibly part of her life, and she part of the life of Great Mop. She took up a plate and looked at the maker's mark. It had come from Stoke-on-Trent, where she had never been. Now it was here, waiting for her to eat off it. 'The Kings of Tarshish shall bring gifts,' she murmured.

As she spoke, she felt something move by her foot. She glanced down and saw a small kitten. It crouched by her foot, biting her shoe-lace, and lashing its tail from side to side. Laura did not like cats; but this creature, so small, so intent, and so ferocious, amused her into kindly feelings. 'How did you come here? Did you come in through the keyhole?' she asked, and bent down to stroke it. Scarcely had she touched its hard little head when it writhed itself round her hand, noiselessly clawing and biting, and kicking with its hind legs. She felt frightened by an attack so fierce and irrational, and her fears increased as she tried to shake off the tiny weight. At last she freed her hand, and looked at it. It was covered with fast-reddening scratches, and as she looked she saw a bright round drop of blood ooze out from one of them. Her heart gave a violent leap, and seemed to drop dead in her bosom. She gripped the back of a chair to steady herself and stared at the kitten. Abruptly pacified, it had curled itself into a ball and fallen asleep. Its lean ribs heaved with a rhythmic tide of sleep. As she stared she saw its pink tongue flicker for one moment over its lips It slept like a suckling.

Not for a moment did she doubt. But so deadly, so complete was the certainty that it seemed to paralyse her powers of understanding, like a snake-bite in the brain. She continued to stare at the kitten, scarcely knowing what it was that she knew. Her heart had begun to beat once more, slowly, slowly; her ears were dizzied with a shrill wall of sound, and her flesh hung on her clammy and unreal. The animal smell that she had noticed when first she entered the room now seemed overwhelmingly rank. It smelt as if walls and floor and ceiling had been smeared with the juice of bruised fennel.

She, Laura Willowes, in England, in the year 1922, had entered into a compact with the Devil. The compact was made, and affirmed, and sealed with the round red seal of her blood. She remembered the woods, she remembered her wild cry for help, and the silence that had followed it, as though in ratification. She heard again the mutter of heavy foliage, foliage dark and heavy as the wings of night birds. 'No! No!' – she heard the brooding voice – 'We will not let you go.' At ease, released from her cares, she had walked homeward. Hedge and coppice and solitary tree, and the broad dustcoloured faces of meadow-sweet and hemlock had watched her go by, knowing. The dusk had closed her in, brooding over her. Every shadow, every deepened grove had observed her from under their brows of obscurity. All knew, all could bear witness. Couched within the wood, sleeping through the long sultry afternoon, had lain the Prince of Darkness; sleeping, or meditating some brooding thunderstorm of his own. Her voice of desperate need had aroused him, his silence had answered her with a pledge. And now, as a sign of the bond between them, he had sent his emissary. It had arrived before her, a rank breath, a harsh black body in her locked room. The kitten was her familiar spirit, that already had greeted its mistress, and sucked her blood.

She shut her eyes and stood very still, hollowing her mind to admit this inconceivable thought. Suddenly she started. There was a voice in the room.

It was the kitten's voice. It stood beside her, mewing plaintively. She turned, and considered it – her familiar. It was the smallest and thinnest kitten that she had ever seen. It was so young that it could barely stand steadily upon its legs. She caught herself thinking that it was too young to be taken from its mother. But the thought was ridiculous. Probably it had no mother, for it was the Devil's kitten, and sucked, not milk, but blood. But for all that, it looked very like any other young starveling of its breed. Its face was peaked and its ribs stood out under the dishevelled fluff of its sides. Its mew was disproportionately piercing and expressive. Strange that anything so small and weak should be the Devil's Officer, plenipotentiary of such a power. Strange that she should stand trembling and amazed before a little rag-and-bone kitten with absurdly large ears.

Its anxious voice besought her, its pale eyes were fixed upon her face. She could not but feel sorry for anything that seemed so defenceless and castaway. Poor little creature, no doubt it missed the Devil, its warm nest in his shaggy flanks, its play with imp companions. Now it had been sent out on its master's business, sent out too young into the world, like a slavey from an Institution. It had no one to look to now but her, and it implored her help, as she but a little while ago had implored its Master's. Her pity overcame her terror. It was no longer her familiar, but a foundling. And it was hungry. Must it have more blood, or would milk do? Milk was more suitable for its tender age. She walked to the table, poured out a saucerful of milk and set it down on the floor. The kitten drank as though it were starving. Crouched by the saucer with dabbled nose, it shut its pale eyes and laid back its ears to lap, while shoots of ecstasy ran down its protuberant spine and stirred the tip of its tail. As Laura watched it the last of her repugnance was overcome. Though she did not like cats she thought that she would like this one. After all, it was pleasant to have some small thing to look after. Many lonely women found great companionship with even quite ordinary cats. This creature could never grow up a beauty, but no doubt it would be intelligent. When it had cleaned the saucer with large final sweeps of its tongue, the kitten looked up at her. 'Poor lamb!' she said, and poured out the rest of the milk. It drank less famishingly now. Its tail lay still, its body relaxed, settling down on to the floor, overcome by the peaceful weight within. At last, having finished its meal, it got up and walked round the room, stretching either hind leg in turn as it walked. Then, without a glance at Laura, it lay down, coiled and uncoiled, scratched itself nonchalantly and fell asleep. She watched it awhile and then picked it up, all limp and unresisting, and settled it in her lap. It scarcely opened its eyes, but burrowing once or twice with its head against her knees resumed its slumber.

Nursing the kitten in her lap Laura sat thinking. Her thoughts were of a different colour now. This trustful contentment, this warmth between her knees, lulled her by example. She had never wavered for an instant from her conviction that she had made a compact with the Devil; now she was growing accustomed to the thought. She perceived that throughout the greater part of her life she had been growing accustomed to it; but insensibly, as people throughout the greater part of their lives grow accustomed to the thought of their death. When it comes, it is a surprise to them. But the surprise does not last long, perhaps but for a minute or two. Her surprise also was wearing off. Quite soon, and she would be able to fold her hands upon it, as the hands of the dead are folded upon their surprised hearts. But her heart still beat, beat at its everyday rate, a small regular pulse impelling her momently forward into the new witch life that lay before her. Since her flesh had already accepted the new order of things, and was proceeding so methodically towards the future, it behoved her, so she thought, to try to readjust her spirit.

She raised her eyes, and looked at her room, the green-painted walls with the chairs sitting silently round. She felt herself inhabiting the empty house. Through the unrevealing square of the window her mind looked at the view. About the empty house was the village, and about the village the hills, neighbourly under their covering of night. Room, house, village, hills encircled her like the rings of a fortification This was her domain, and it was to keep this inviolate that she had made her compact with the Devil. She did not know what the price might be, but she was sure of the purchase. She need not fear Titus now, nor any of the Willoweses. They could not drive her out, or enslave her spirit any more, nor shake her possession of the place she had chosen While she lived her solitudes were hers inalienably; she and the kitten, the witch and the familial, would live on at Great Mop, growing old together, and hearing the owls hoot from the winter trees. And after? Mirk! But what else had there ever been? Those green grassy hills in the churchyard were too high to be seen over. What man can stand on their summit and look beyond?

She felt neither fear nor disgust. A witch of but a few hours' standing she rejected with the scorn of the initiate all the bugaboo surmises of the public. She looked with serene curiosity at the future, and saw it but little altered from what she had hoped and planned. If she had been called upon to decide in cold blood between being an aunt and being a witch, she might have been overawed by habit and the cowardice of compunction. But in the moment of election, under the stress and turmoil of the hunted Lolly as under a covering of darkness, the true Laura had settled it all unerringly. She had known where to turn. She had been like the girl in the fairy tale whose godmother gave her a little nutshell box and told her to open it in the hour of utter distress. Unsurmised by others, and half forgotten by the girl, the little nutshell box abided its time; and in the hour of utter distress it opened of itself. So, unrealised, had Laura been carrying her talisman in her pocket. She was a witch by vocation. Even in the old days of Lady Place the impulse had stirred in her. What else had set her upon her long solitary walks, her quests for powerful and forgotten herbs, her brews and distillations? In London she had never had the heart to take out her still. More urgent for being denied this innocent service, the ruling power of her life had assaulted her with dreams and intimations, calling her imagination out from the warm safe room to wander in darkened fields and by desolate sea-bords, through marshes and fens, and along the outskirts of brooding woods. It had haled her to Wapping and to the Jews' Burying Ground, and then, ironically releasing her, had left her to mourn and find her way back to Apsley Terrace. How she had come to Great Mop she could not say; whether it was of her own will, or whether, exchanging threatenings and mockeries for sweet persuasions, Satan had at last taken pity upon her bewilderment, leading her by the hand into the flower-shop in the Moscow Road; but from the moment of her arrival there he had never been far off. Sure of her – she supposed – he had done little for nine months but watch her. Near at hand but out of sight the loving huntsman couched in the woods, following her with his eyes. But all the time, whether couched in the woods or hunting among the hills, he drew closer. He was hidden in the well when she threw in the map and the guide-book. He sat in the oven, teaching her what power she might have over the shapes of men. He followed her and Mr. Saunter up and down between the henhouses. He was nearest of all upon the night when she climbed Cubbey Ridge, so near then that she acknowledged his presence and was afraid. That night, indeed, he must have been within a hand's-breadth of her. But her fear had kept him at bay, or else he had not chosen to take her just then, preferring to watch until he could overcome her mistrust and lure her into his hand. For Satan is not only a huntsman. His interest in mankind is that of a skilful and experienced naturalist. Even human sportsmen at the end of their span sometimes declare that to potter about in the woods is more amusing than to sit behind a butt and shoot driven grouse. And Satan, who has hunted from eternity, a little jaded moreover by the success of his latest organised Flanders battue, might well feel that his interest in a Solitary Snipe like Laura was but sooner or later to measure the length of her nose. Yet hunt he must; it is his destiny, and whether he hunts with a gun or a butterfly net, sooner or later the chase must end. All finalities, whether good or evil, bestow a feeling of relief; and now, understanding how long the chase had lasted, Laura felt a kind of satisfaction at having been popped into the bag.

She was distracted from these interesting thoughts by the sounds of footsteps. The kitten heard them too, and sat up, yawning. The Leaks coming back from their lecture, thought Laura. But it was Titus. Inserting his head and shoulders through the window he asked if he could come in and borrow some milk.

'I haven't any milk,' said Laura, 'but come in all the same.'

She began to tickle the kitten behind the ears in order to reassure it. By lamplight Titus's head seemed even nearer to the ceiling, it was a relief to her sense of proportion when he sat down. His milk, he explained, the jugful which Mrs. Garland left on the sitting-room table for his nightly Ovaltine, had curdled into a sort of unholy junket. This he attributed to popular education, and the spread of science among dairy-farmers; in other words, Mr. Dodbury had overdone the preservative.

'I don't think it's science,' said Laura. 'More likely to be the weather. It was very sultry this afternoon.'

'I saw you starting out. I had half a mind to come with you, but it was too hot to be a loving nephew. Where did you go?'

'Up to the windmill.'

'Did you find the wind?'

'No.'

'You weren't going in the direction of the windmill when I saw you.'

'No. I changed my mind. About the milk,' she continued (Titus had come for milk. Perhaps, being reminded that he had come in vain, he would go. She was growing sleepy): 'I'm sorry, but I have none left. I gave it all to the kitten.' 'I've been remarking the kitten. He's new, isn't he? You ugly little devil!'

The kitten lay on her knees quite quietly. It regarded Titus with its pale eyes, and blinked indifferently. It was only waiting for him to go, Laura thought, to fall asleep again.

'Where has it come from? A present from the water-butt?'

'I don't know. I found it here when I came back for supper.'

'It's a plain-headed young Grimalkin. Still, I should keep it if I were you. It will bring you luck.'

'I don't think one has much option about keeping a cat,' said Laura. 'If it wants to stay with me it shall.'

'It looks settled enough. Do keep it, Aunt Lolly. A woman looks her best with a cat on her knees.'

Laura bowed.

'What will you call it?'

Into Laura's memory came a picture she had seen long ago in one of the books at Lady Place. The book was about the persecution of the witches, and the picture was a woodcut of Matthew Hopkins the witch-finder. Wearing a large hat he stood among a coven of witches, bound cross-legged upon their stools. Their confessions came out of their mouths upon scrolls. 'My imp's name is Ilemauzar,' said one; and another imp at the bottom of the page, an alert, ill-favoured cat, so lean and muscular that it looked like a skinned hare, was called Vinegar Tom.

'I shall call it Vinegar,' she answered.

'Vinegar!' said Titus. 'How do you like your name?'

The kitten pricked up its ears. It sprang from Laura's knee and began to fence with Titus's shadow, feinting and leaping back. Laura watched it a little apprehensively, but it did him no harm. It had awakened in a playful frame of mind after its long sleep, that was all. When Titus had departed it followed Laura to her bedroom, and as she undressed it danced round her, patting at her clothes as they fell.

In the morning the kitten roused her by mewing to be let out. She awoke from a profound and dreamless sleep. It took her a little time to realise that she had a kitten in her bedroom, a kitten of no ordinary kind. However it was behaving quite like an ordinary kitten now, so she got out of bed and let it out by the back door. It was early; no one was stirring. The kitten disappeared with dignity among the cabbages, and Laura turned her thoughts backward to the emotions of overnight. She tried to recall them, but could not; she could only recall the fact that overnight she had felt them. The panic that then had shaken her flesh was no more actual than a last winter's gale. It had been violent enough while it lasted, an invisible buffeting, a rending of life from its context. But now her memory presented it to her as a cold slab of experience, like a slab of pudding that had lain all night solidifying in the larder. This was no matter. Her terror had been an incident; it had no bearing upon hei future, could she now recall it to life it would have no message for her. But she regretted her inability to recapture the mood that had followed upon it, when she sat still and thought so wisely about Satan. Those meditations had seemed to her of profound import. She had sat at her Master's feet, as it were, admitted to intimacy, and gaining the most valuable insight into his character. But that was gone too. Her thoughts, recalled, seemed to be of the most commonplace nature, and she felt that she knew very little about the Devil.

Meanwhile there was the kitten, an earnest that she should know more.

'Vinegar!' she called, and heard its answer, a drumming scramble among the cabbage leaves. She wished that Vinegar would impart some of his mind to her instead of being so persistently and genially kittenish. But he was a familiar, no doubt of it. And she was a witch, the inheritrix of aged magic, spells rubbed smooth with long handling, and the mistress of strange powers that got into Titus's milk-jug. For no doubt that was the beginning, and a very good beginning, too. Well begun is half-done; she could see Titus bending over his suit-case. The Willowes tradition was very intolerant of pease under its mattress.

Though she tried to think clearly about the situation – grapple, she remembered, had been Caroline's unpleasantly strenuous word – her attention kept sidling off to other things: the sudden oblique movements of the water-drops that glistened on the cabbage leaves, or the affinity between the dishevelled brown hearts of the sunflowers and Mrs. Leak's scrubbing-brush, propped up on the kitchen window-sill. It must have rained heavily during the night. The earth was moist and swelled, and the air so fresh that it made her yawn. Her limbs were heavy, and the contentment of the newly-awakened was upon her. All night she had bathed in nothingness, and now she was too recently emerged from that absolving tide to take much interest in what lay upon its banks. Her eyelids began to droop, and calling the kitten she went back to bed again and soon fell asleep.

She was asleep when Mrs. Leak brought her morning tea.

Mrs. Leak said: 'Did the thunder keep you awake, miss?'

Laura shook her head. 'I never even heard it.'

Mrs. Leak looked much astonished. 'It's well to have a good conscience,' she remarked.

Laura stretched herself, sat up in bed, and began to tell Mrs. Leak about the kitten. This seemed to be her real awakening. The other was a dream.

Mrs. Leak was quite prepared to welcome the kitten; that was, provided her old Jim made no unpleasantness Jim was not Mr. Leak, but a mottled marmalade cat, very old and rather shabby. Laura could not imagine him making any unpleasantness, but Mrs. Leak estimated his character rather differently. Jim thought himself quite a Great I Am, she said.

After breakfast Laura and Vinegar were called into the kitchen for the ceremony of introduction. Jim was doing a little washing. His hind leg was stuck straight up, out of the way, while he attended to the pit of his stomach. Nothing could have been more suitable than Vinegar's modest and deferential approach. Jim gave him one look and went on licking. Mrs. Leak said that all would be well between them; Jim always kept himself to himself, but she could see that the old cat had taken quite a fancy to Miss Willowes's kitten. She promised Vinegar some of Jim's rabbit for dinner. Mrs. Leak did not hold the ordinary view of country people that cats must fend for themselves. 'They're as thoughtful as we,' she said. 'Why should they eat mouse unless they want to?' She was continually knocking at the parlour door with tit-bits for Vinegar, but she was scrupulous that Laura should bestow them with her own hand.

Since Titus had come to Great Mop Laura had seen little of Mrs. Leak. Mrs. Leak knew what good manners were; she had not been a housemaid at Lazzard Court for nothing. Taken separately, either Titus or his aunt might be human beings, but in conjunction they became gentry. Mrs. Leak remembered her position and withdrew to it, firmly. Laura saw this and was sorry.

She made several attempts to persuade Mrs. Leak out from behind her white apron, but nothing came of them, and she knew that while Titus was in the village nothing would. Not that Mrs. Leak did not like Titus; she approved of him highly; and it was exactly her approval that made her barricade of respect so insuperable. But where Laura had failed, the kitten succeeded. From the moment that Jim sanctioned her kindly opinion of him, Mrs. Leak began to thaw. Laura knew better than to make a fuss over this turn in the situation; she took a leaf out of the Devil's book and lay low, waiting for a decisive advance; and presently it came. Mrs. Leak asked if Miss Willowes would care to come out for a stroll one evening; it was pleasant to get a breath of air before bedtime. Miss Willowes would like nothing better; that very evening would suit her if Mrs. Leak had nothing else to do. Mrs. Leak said that she would get the washing-up done as soon as possible, and after that she would be at Miss Willowes's disposal. However, it was nearly half-past ten before Mrs. Leak knocked on the parlour door. Laura had ceased to expect her, supposing that Mr. Leak or some household accident had claimed her, but she was quite as ready to go out for a walk as to go to bed, and Mrs. Leak made no reference to the lateness of the hour. Indeed, according to the Great Mop standard, the hour was not particularly late. Although the night was dark, Laura noticed that quite a number of the inhabitants were standing about in the street

They walked down the road in silence as far as the milestone, and turned into the track that went up the hillside and past the wood. Others had turned that way also. The gate stood open, and voices sounded ahead. It was then that Laura guessed the truth, and turned to her companion.

'Where are you taking me?' she said. Mrs. Leak made no answer, but in the darkness she took hold of Laura's hand. There was no need for further explanation. They were going to the Witches' Sabbath. Mrs. Leak was a witch too; a matronly witch like Agnes Sampson, she would be Laura's chaperone. The night was full of voices Padding rustic footsteps went by them in the dark. When they had reached the brow of the hill a faint continuous sound, resembling music, was borne towards them by the light wind. Laura remembered how young Billy Thomas, suffering from toothache, had played all night upon his mouth-organ. She laughed. Mrs. Leak squeezed her hand.

The meeting-place was some way off, by the time they reached it Laura's eyes had grown accustomed to the darkness. She could see a crowd of people walking about in a large field; lights of some sort were burning under a hedge, and one or two paper garlands were looped over the trees. When she first caught sight of them, the assembled witches and warlocks seemed to be dancing, but now the music had stopped and they were just walking about. There was something about their air of disconnected jollity which reminded Laura of a Primrose League gala and fête. A couple of bullocks watched the Sabbath from an adjoining field.

Laura was denied the social gift, she had never been good at enjoying parties. But this, she hoped, would be a different and more exhilarating affair. She entered the field in a most propitious frame of mind, which not even Mr. Gurdon, wearing a large rosette like a steward's and staring rudely and searchingly at each comer before he allowed them to pass through the gate, was able to check.

'Old Goat!' exclaimed Mrs. Leak in a voice of contemptuous amusement after they had passed out of Mr. Gurdon's hearing. 'He thinks he can boss us here, just as he does in the village.'

'Is Mr. Jones here?' inquired Laura.

Mrs. Leak shook her head and laughed.

'Mr. Gurdon doesn't allow him to come.'

'I suppose he doesn't think it suitable for a clergyman.'

Perhaps it was as well that Mr. Gurdon had such strict views. In spite of the example of Mr. Lowis, that old reading parson, it might be a little awkward if Mr. Jones were allowed to attend the Sabbath.

But that apparently was not the reason. Mrs. Leak was beginning to explain when she broke off abruptly, coughed in a respectful way, and dropped a deep curtsey. Before them stood an old lady, carrying herself like a queen, and wearing a mackintosh that would have disgraced a tinker's drab. She acknowledged Mrs. Leak's curtsey with an inclination of the head, and turned to Laura

'I am Miss Larpent. And you, I think, must be Miss Willowes.'

The voice that spoke was clear as a small bell and colourless as if time had bleached it of every human feeling save pride. The hand that rested in Laura's was light as a bird's claw; a fine glove encased it like a membrane, and through the glove Laura felt the slender bonef and the sharp-faceted rings.

'Long ago,' continued Miss Larpent, 'I had the pleasure of meeting your great-uncle, Commodore Willowes.'

Good heavens, thought Laura in a momentary confusion, was great-uncle Demetrius a warlock? For Miss Larpent was so perfectly witchlike that it seemed scarcely possible that she should condescend to ordinary gentlemen.

Apparently Miss Larpent could read Laura's thoughts.

'At Cowes,' she added, reassuringly.

Laura raised her eyes to answer, but Miss Larpent had disappeared. Where she had stood, stood Miss Carloe, mincing and bridling, as though she would usurp the other's gentility. Over her face she wore a spotted veil. Recognising Laura she put on an air of delighted surprise and squeaked like a bat, and immediately she too edged away and was lost in the darkness.

Then a young man whom she did not know came up to Laura and put his arm respectfully round her waist. She found herself expected to dance. She could not hear any music, but she danced as best she could, keeping time to the rhythm of his breath upon her cheek. Their dance was short, she supposed she had not acquitted herself to her partner's satisfaction, for after a few turns he released her, and left her standing by the hedge. Not a word had passed between them. Laura felt that she ought to say something, but she could not think of a suitable opening. It was scarcely possible to praise the floor.

A familiar discouragement began to settle upon her spirits. In spite of her hopes she was not going to enjoy herself. Even as a witch, it seemed, she was doomed to social failure, and her first Sabbath was not going to open livelier vistas than were opened by her first ball. She remembered her dancing days in Somerset, Hunt Balls, and County Balls in the draughty Assembly Rooms. With the best intentions she had never managed to enjoy them. The first hour was well enough, but after that came increasing listlessness and boredom j the effort, when one danced again with the same partner, not to say the same things, combined with the obligation to say something rather like them, the control of eyelids, the conversion of yawns into smiles, the humbling consciousness that there was nothing to look forward to except the drive home. That was pleasant, and so was the fillip of supper at the drive's end, and the relief of yielding at last to an unfeigned hunger and sleepiness. But these were by-blow joys, of the delights for which balls are ordained she knew nothing.

She watched the dancers go by and wondered what the enchantment was which they felt and she could not. What made them come out in the middle of the night, loop paper garlands over the trees, light a row of candles in the ditch, and then, friends and enemies and indifférents, go bumping round on the rough grass? That fatal comparison with the Primrose League recurred to her. She was not entertained, so she blamed the entertainment. But the fault lay with her, she had never been good at parties, she had not got the proper Sabbath-keeping spirit. Miss Larpent was enjoying herself; Laura saw the bonnet whisk past. But doubtless Miss Larpent had enjoyed herself at Cowes.

These depressing thoughts were interrupted by red-haired Emily, who came spinning from her partner's arms, seized hold of Laura and carried her back into the dance. Laura liked dancing with Emily; the pasty-faced and anaemic young slattern whom she had seen dawdling about the village danced with a fervour that annihilated every misgiving. They whirled faster and faster, fused together like two suns that whirl and blaze in a single destruction. A strand of the red hair came undone and brushed across Laura's face. The contact made her tingle from head to foot. She shut her eyes and dived into obliviousness – with Emily for a partner she could dance until the gunpowder ran out of the heels of her boots. Alas! this happy ending was not to be, for at the height of their performance Emily was snatched away by Mr. Jowl, the horse-doctor. Laura opened her eyes and saw the pale face disappearing in the throng as the moon sinks into the clouds.

Emily was in great request, and no wonder. Like a torch she was handed on from one to another, and every mutation shook down some more hair. The Sabbath was warming up nicely now, everyone was jigging it, even Laura. For a while Mrs. Leak kept up a semblance of chaperonage. Suddenly appearing at Laura's elbow she would ask her if she were enjoying herself, and glancing at her would slip away before she could answer. Or with vague gestures she indicated some evasively bowing partner, male or female; and silently Laura would give her hand and be drawn into the dance, presently to be relinquished or carried off by someone else.

The etiquette of a Sabbath appeared to consist of one rule only: to do nothing for long. Partners came and went, figures and conformations were in a continual flux. Sometimes the dancers were coupled, sometimes they jigged in a circle round some specially agile performer, sometimes they all took hands and galloped about the field. Half-way through a very formal quadrille presided over by the Misses Larpent they fell abruptly to playing Fox and Geese. In spite of Mr. Gurdon's rosette there was no Master of Ceremonies. A single mysterious impulse seemed to govern the company. They wheeled and manoeuvred like a flock of starlings.

After an hour or two of this Laura felt dizzy and bewildered. Taking advantage of the general lack of formality she tore herself from Mr. Gurdon's arms, not to dance with another, but to slip away and sit quietly in the hedge.

She wondered where the music came from. She had heard it quite clearly as she came over the hill, but upon entering the field she had lost it. Now as she watched the others she heard it once more. When they neared it grew louder, when they retreated into the darkness it faded with them, as though the sound issued from the dancers themselves, and hung, a droning exhalation, above their heads. It was an odd kind of music, a continuous high shapeless blurr of sound. It was something like mosquitoes in a hot bedroom, and something like a distant threshing machine. But beside this, it had a faintly human quality, a metallic breathing as of trombones marking the measure; and when the dancers took hands and revolved in a leaping circle the music leaped and pounded with them, so much like the steam-organ music of a merry-go-round that for a moment Laura thought that they were riding on horses and dragons, bobbing up and down on crested dragons with heads like cocks, and horses with blood-red nostrils.

The candles burnt on in the dry ditch. Though the boughs of the thorn-trees moved above them and grated in the night-wind, the candle flames flowed steadily upwards. Thus lit from below, the dancers seemed of more than human stature, their bodies extending into the darkness as if in emulation of their gigantic upcast shadows. The air was full of the smell of bruised grass.

Mrs. Leak had forgotten Laura now. She was dancing the Highland Schottische with a lean young man whose sleeves were rolled up over his tattooed forearms The nails in his boots shone in the candle-light, and a lock of hair hung over his eye. Mrs. Leak danced very well. Her feet flickered to and fro as nimbly as a tongue. At the turn of the figure she tripped forward to be caught up and swung round on the young man's arm. Though her feet were off the ground they twitched with the movements of the dance, and set down again they took up the uninterrupted measure Laura watched her with admiration. Even at a Witches' Sabbath Mrs. Leak lost none of her respectability. Her white apron was scarcely crumpled, she was as self-contained as a cat watching a mouse, and her eyes dwelt upon the young man's face as though she were listening to a sermon.

She preserved her dignity better than some of the others did. Mr. Gurdon stood by himself, stamping his foot and tossing his head, more like the farmer's bull than ever. Miss Carloe was begging people to look at the hole in her leg where the hedgehog sucked her; and red-haired Emily, half-naked and holding a candle in either hand, danced round a tree, curtseying to it, her mouth fixed in a breathless corpse-like grin.

Miss Minnie and Miss Jane had also changed their demeanour for the worse. They sat a little retired from the dancers, tearing up a cold grouse and gossiping with Mrs. Dewey the midwife. A horrible curiosity stretched their skinny old necks. Miss Minnie had forgotten to gnaw her grouse, she leant forward, her hand covered the lower half of her face to conceal the workings of her mouth. Miss Jane listened as eagerly, and questioned the midwife. But at the answers she turned away with coquettish shudders, pretending to stop her ears, or threatening to slap her sister with a bone.

Laura averted her eyes. She wriggled herself a little further into the hedge. Once again the dancers veered away to the further side of the field, their music retreating with them. She hoped they would stay away, for their proximity was disturbing. They aroused in her neither fear nor disgust, but when they came close, and she felt their shadows darkening above her head, a nameless excitement caught hold of her. As they departed, heaviness took its place. She was not in the least sleepy and yet several times she found herself astray from her thoughts, as though she were falling asleep in a train. She wondered what time it was and looked up to consult the stars. But a featureless cloud covered the sky.

Laura resigned herself. There was nothing to do but to wait, though what she waited for she did not know: whether at length Mrs. Leak would come, like a chaperone from the supper-room, and say: 'Well, my dear, I really must take you home' – or if, suddenly, at the first cock-crow, all the company would rise up in the air, a darkening bevy, and disperse, and she with them.

She was roused by a shrill whistle. The others heard it too. Miss Minnie and Miss Jane scrambled up and hurried across the field, outdistancing Mrs. Dewey, who followed them panting for breath and twitching her skirts over the rough ground. The music had stopped. Laura saw all the witches and warlocks jostling each other, and pressing into a circle. She wondered what was happening now. Whatever it was, it seemed to please and excite them a great deal, for she could hear them all laughing and talking at once. Some newcomer, she supposed – for their behaviour was that of welcome. Now the newcomer must be making a speech, for they all became silent: a successful speech, for the silence was broken by acclamations, and bursts of laughter.

'Of course!' said Laura. 'It must be Satan!'As she spoke she saw the distant group turn and with one accord begin running towards where she sat. She got up; she felt frightened, for their advance was like a stampede of animals, and she feared that they would knock her down and trample her underfoot. The first runner had already swooped upon her, she felt herself encompassed, caught hold of, and carried forward. Voices addressed her, but she did not understand what was said. She gathered that she was being encouraged and congratulated, as though the neglectful assembly had suddenly decided to make much of the unsuccessful guest. Presently she found herself between Mrs. Leak and red-haired Emily. Each held an arm. Mrs. Leak patted her encouragingly, and Emily whispered rapidly, incoherently, in her ear. They were quite close to the newcomer, Satan, if it were he, who was talking to Miss Minnie and Miss Jane. Laura looked at him. She could see him quite clearly, for those who stood round had taken up the candles to light him. He was standing with his back to her, speaking with great animation to the old ladies, bowing, and fidgeting his feet. As he spoke he threw out his hands, and his whole lean, lithe body seemed to be scarcely withheld from breaking into a dance. Laura saw Miss Jane point at her, and the stranger turned sharply round.

She saw his face. For a moment she thought that he was a Chinaman; then she saw that he was wearing a mask. The candle-light shone full upon it, but so fine and slight was the modelling that scarcely a shadow marked the indentations of cheek and jaw. The narrow eyes, the slanting brows, the small smiling mouth had a vivid innocent inexpressiveness. It was like the face of a very young girl. Alert and immobile the mask regarded her. And she, entranced, stared back at this imitation face that outwitted all perfections of flesh and blood. It was lifeless, lifeless! But below it, in the hollow of the girlish throat, she saw a flicker of life, a small regular pulse, small and regular as though a pearl necklace slid by under the skin. Mincing like a girl, the masked young man approached her, and as he approached the others drew back and left her alone. With secretive and undulating movements he came to her side. The lifeless face was near her own and through the slits in the mask the unseen eyes surveyed her. Suddenly she felt upon her cheeks a cold darting touch. With a fine tongue like a serpent's he had licked her right cheek, close to the ear. She started back, but found his hands detaining her.

'How are you enjoying your first Sabbath, Miss Willowes?' he said.

'Not at all,' answered Laura, and turned her back on him.

Without glancing to left or right she walked out of the field, and the dancers made way for her in silence. She was furious at the affront, raging at Satan, at Mrs. Leak, at Miss Larpent, with the unreasoning anger of a woman who has allowed herself to be put in a false position. This was what came of attending Sabbaths, or rather, this was what came of submitting her good sense to politeness. Hours ago her instinct had told her that she was not going to enjoy herself. If she had asserted herself and gone home then, this odious and petty insult would never have happened. But she had stayed on, deferring to a public opinion that was not concerned whether she stayed or went, stayed on just as she used to stay on at balls, stayed on to be treated like a silly girl who at the end of a mechanical flirtation is kissed behind a palm.

Anyway, she was out of it now. Her feet had followed the windings of a little path, which crossed a ditch by a plank bridge: it passed through a belt of woodland, and led her out on to a space of common that sloped away into the darkness. Here she sat down and spread out her palms upon the cool turf.

She had been insulted and made a mock of. But for all that she did not feel truly humiliated. Rather, she was filled with a delighted and scornful surprise at the ease with which she had avenged her dignity. The mask floated before her eyes, inscrutable as ever, and she thought no more of it than of an egg-shell that she could crush between her finger and thumb. The Powers of Darkness, then, were no more fearful than a herd of bullocks in a field? Once round upon them and the sniffing encumbering horde made off, a scramble of ungainly rumps and foolish tails.

It had been a surprising night. And long, endlessly long, and not ended yet. She yawned, and felt hungry. She fancied herself at home, cutting large crumbling slices from the loaf in the cupboard, and spreading them with a great deal of butter and the remains of the shrimp paste. But she did not know where she was, and it was too dark to venture homewards with no sense of direction. She grew impatient with the night and strained her ears for the sound of cock-crow. As if her imperious will had wrenched aside the covering of cloud, a faint glimmer delineated part of the horizon. Moonset or sunrise, westerly or easterly she did not know; but as she watched it doubtfully, thinking that it must be moonset, for it seemed to dwindle rather than increase, a breeze winnowed the air, and looking round her she saw on every side the first beginnings of light.

Sitting up, her hunger and sleepiness forgotten, and all the disappointments and enigmas of the Sabbath dismissed from her mind, she watched the spectacle of the dawn. Soon she was able to recognise her surroundings, she knew the place well, it was here that she had met the badger. The slope before her was dotted with close-fitting juniper bushes, and presently she saw a rabbit steal out from one of these, twitch its ears, and scamper off.

The cloud which covered the sky was no longer a solid thing. It was rising, and breaking up into swirls of vapour that yielded to the wind. The growing day washed them with silver. Every moment the web of cloud seemed to rise higher and higher, as though borne upward by a rising tide of light. The rooks flew up cawing from the wood. Presently she heard the snap of a dead twig. Somebody was astir. Whistling to himself, a man came out of the wood. He walked with a peculiarly slow and easy gait, and he had a stick in his hand, an untrimmed rod pulled from the wood. He switched at the head of a tall thistle, and Laura saw the dew fly off the astonished blossom. Seeing her, he stopped short, as though he did not wish to intrude on her. He showed no surprise that she should be sitting on the hillside, waiting for the sun to rise. She smiled at him, grateful for his good manners, and also quite pleased to see a reasonable being again; and emboldened by this, he smiled also, and approached.

'You are up very early, Miss Willowes?

She did not recognise him, but that was no reason why he should not recognise her. She thought he must be a gamekeeper, for he wore gaiters and a corduroy coat. His face was brown and wrinkled, and his teeth were as white and even as a dog's. Laura liked his appearance. He had a pleasant, rather detached air, which suited well with the early morning. She said:

'I have been up all night?

There was no inquisitiveness in his look; and when he expressed the hope that she felt none the worse for it, he spoke without servility or covert amusement.

'I liked it very much,' said Laura. Her regard for truth made her add: 'Particularly when it began to be light. I was growing rather bored before then?

'Some ladies would feel afraid,' said he.

'I'm not afraid when I'm alone,' she answered. 'I lived in the country when I was a girl.'

He bowed his head assentingly. Something in his manner implied that he knew this already. Perhaps he had heard about her in the village.

'It's pleasant to be in the country again,' she continued. 'I like Great Mop very much.'

'I hope you will stay here, Miss Willowes.'

'I hope so too.'

She spoke a little sadly. In this unaccustomed hour her soul was full of doubts. She wondered if, having flouted the Sabbath, she were still a witch, or whether, her power being taken from her, she would become the prey of a healthy and untroubled Titus. And being faint for want of food and want of sleep, she foreboded the worst.

'Yes, you must stay here. It would be a pity to go now.'

Laura nearly said, 'I have nowhere to go,' but a dread of exile came over her like a salt wave, and she could not trust herself to speak to this kind man. He came nearer and said:

'Remember, Miss Willowes, that I shall always be very glad to help you. You have only to ask me.'

'But where shall I find you?' she asked, too much impressed by the kindness of his words to think them strange.

'You will always find me in the wood,' he answered, and touching his cap he walked away. She heard the noise of swishing branches and the scuff of feet among dead leaves growing fainter as he went further into the wood.

She decided not to go back just yet. A comfortable drowsiness settled down upon her with the first warmth of the risen sun.

Her mind dwelt upon the words just spoken. The promise had been given in such sober earnestness that she had accepted it without question, seeing nothing improbable in the idea that she should require the help of a strange gamekeeper, or that he should undertake to give it. She thought that people might be different in the early morning; less shy, like the rabbits that were playing round her, more open-hearted, and simpler of speech. In any case, she was grateful to the stranger for his goodwill. He had known that she wanted to stay on at Great Mop, he had told her that she must do so. It was the established country courtesy, the invitation to take root. But he must have meant what he said, for seeing her troubled he had offered to help. Perhaps he was married; and if Mrs. Leak, offended, would keep her no longer, she might lodge with him and his wife in their cottage, a cottage in a dell among the beechwoods. He had said that he lived in the woods. She began to picture her life in such a cottage, thinking that it would be even better than lodging in the village. She imagined her whitewashed bedroom full of moving green shades; the wood-smoke curling up among the trees; the majestic arms, swaying above her while she slept, and plumed with snow in winter.

The trees behind her murmured consolingly; she reclined upon the sound. 'Remember, Miss Willowes' … 'Remember,' murmured the trees, swaying their boughs muffled with heavy foliage. She remembered, and understood. When he came out of the wood, dressed like a gamekeeper, and speaking so quietly and simply, Satan had come to renew his promise and to reassure her. He had put on this shape that she might not fear him. Or would he have her to know that to those who serve him he appears no longer as a hunter, but as a guardian? This was the real Satan. And as for the other, whom her spirit had so impetuously disowned, she had done well to disown him, for he was nothing but an impostor, a charlatan, a dummy.

Her doubts were laid to rest, and she walked back through the fields, picking mushrooms as she went. As she approached the village she heard Mr. Saunter's cocks crowing, and saw the other cock, forever watchful, forever silent, spangle in the sun above the church tower. The churchyard yews cast long shadows like open graves. Behind those white curtains slumbered Mr. Jones, and dreamed, perhaps, of the Sabbath which he was not allowed to attend.

As Laura passed through Mrs. Leak's garden she remembered her first morning as a witch when she had gone out to give the kitten a run. The sunflowers had been cut off and given to the hens, but the scrubbing-brush was still propped on the kitchen window-sill. That was three weeks ago. And Titus, like the scrubbing-brush, was still there.

During those three weeks Titus had demanded a great deal of support; in fact, being a witchaunt was about twice as taxing as being an ordinary aunt, and if she had not known that the days were numbered she could scarcely have endured them.

At her nephew's request she made veils of butter-muslin weighted with blue beads to protect his food and drink. Titus insisted that the beads should be blue: blue was the colour of the Immaculate Conception; and as pious Continental mothers dedicate their children, so he would dedicate his milk and hope for the best. But no blue beads were to be found in the village, so Laura had to walk into Barleighs for them. Titus was filled with gratitude, he came round on purpose to thank her and stayed to tea.

He was no sooner gone than Mrs. Garland arrived. Mrs. Garland had seen the veils. She hoped that Mr. Willowes didn't think she was to blame for the milk going sour. She could assure Miss Willowes that the jugs were mopped out with boiling water morning and evening. For her part, she couldn't understand it at all. She was always anxious to give satisfaction, she said; but her manner suggested less anxiety to give than to receive. Laura soothed Mrs. Garland, and sat down to wait for Mr. Dodbury. However, Mr. Dodbury contented himself with frowning at that interfering young Willowes's aunt, and turning the bull into the footpath field. Laura thought that the bull frowned too.

Though veiled in butter-muslin, the milk continued to curdle. Titus came in to say that he'd had an idea; in future, he would rely upon condensed milk out of a tin. Which sort did Aunt Lolly recommend? And would she make him a kettle-holder? Apparently tinned milk could resist the Devil, for all was peace until Titus gashed his thumb on the raw edge of a tin. In spite of Laura's first aid the wound festered, and for several days Titus wore a sling. Triumphant over pain he continued the Life of Fuseli. But the wounded thumb being a righthand thumb, the triumph involved an amanuensis. Laura hated ink, she marvelled that any one should have the constancy to write a whole book. She thought of Paradise Lost with a shudder, for it required even more constancy to write someone else's book. Highly as she rated the sufferings of Milton's daughters, she rated her own even higher, for she did not suppose that they had to be forever jumping up and down to light the poet's cigarette; and blank verse flowed, flowed majestically, she understood, from his lips, whereas Titus dictated in prose, which was far harder to punctuate.

Nor did it flow. Titus was not feeling at his best He hated small bothers, and of late he had been seethed alive in them. Every day something went wrong, some fiddle-faddle little thing. All his ingenuity was wasted in circumvention; he had none left for Fuseli.

Anyhow, dictation was only fit for oil-kings! He jumped up and dashed about the room with a fly-flap. Fly-flapping was a manly indoor sport, especially if one observed all the rules. The ceiling was marked out in squares like a chess-board, and while they stayed in their squares the flies could not be attacked. The triangle described by the blue vase, the pink vase, and the hanging lamp was a Yellowstone Park, and so was the King's Face, a difficult ruling, but Titus had decided that of two evils it was more tolerable that the royal countenance should be crawled over by flies than assaulted by the subject. All this from a left-handed adversary – the flies had nothing to complain of, in his opinion. Laura owned his generosity, and sat, when she could, in the Yellowstone Park.

By the time Titus had recovered the use of his right hand the flies had lost their sanctuaries one by one, and could not even call the King's Face their own. They swarmed in his sittingroom, attracted, Mrs. Garland supposed, by the memory of that nasty foreign cheese Mr. Willowes's Mr. Humphries had brought with him when he came to stay. They swarmed in his bedroom also, and that – Mrs. Garland said – was what brought in the bats. Laura told Titus the belief that if a bat once entangles itself in a woman's flowing hair there is no remedy but to cut away hair and bat together. Titus turned pale. That afternoon he went up to London to visit his hairdresser, and returned with hair cropped like a convict's.

All this had unsettled her victim a good deal; but it had not unseated him, and meanwhile it was sufficiently unsettling for her. So far, she thought, the scheme and its execution had been the kitten's – she could recognise Vinegar's playful methods. She gave him credit for doing his best. But he was young and inexperienced, this was probably his first attempt at serious persecution; it was not to be wondered at if his methods were a little sketchy. Now that the Devil had taken matters into his own hands – and of this she felt assured – all would soon be well. Well for her, well for Titus. Really, it was time that poor boy was released from his troubles. She felt complete confidence in the Devil, a confidence that the kitten had never inspired. There was a tinge of gratuitous malice in Vinegar's character; he was, as one says, rather a cat. She suspected him of meditating a scratch which would give Titus blood-poisoning. She remembered with uneasiness what cats are said to do to sleeping infants, and every night she was careful to imprison Vinegar in her bedroom, a useless precaution since he had come in by the keyhole and might as easily go out by it. The Devil would get rid of Titus more speedily, more kindly (he had no reason to be anything but kind: she could not imagine Titus being of the smallest interest to Satan), more economically. There would be no catastrophe, no pantechnicon displays of flood or fire. He would proceed discreetly and surely, like a gamekeeper going his rounds by night; he would remove Titus as imperturbably as Dunlop had removed the beech-leaf. She could sit back quite comfortably now, and wait for it to happen.

When Titus next appeared and complained that he had been kept awake for two nights running by a mouse gnawing rhe leg of his bedstead, Laura was most helpful. They went to Mrs. Trumpet's to buy a mouse-trap, but as Mrs. Trumpet only kept cheese they walked very pleasantly by field-paths into Barleighs, where Denby's stores had a larger range of groceries. During their walk Titus recalled anecdotes illustrative of mice from Soup from a Sausage Peg, and propounded a scheme for defending his bed by a catskin valance. The day was fine, and at intervals Titus would stop and illustrate the landscape with possessive gestures.

He was particularly happy. He had not enjoyed himself so much for some time. The milk and the mice and the flies had checked his spirits; he was not doing justice to Fuseli, and when he went out for long encouraging walks an oppressed feeling went with him. Twice or thrice he had felt horribly frightened, though at what he could not tell. The noise of two iron hurdles grating against each other in the wind, a dead tree with branches that looked like antlers, the stealthy movement of the sun towards the horizon: quite ordinary things like these were able to disquiet him.

He fell into the habit of talking aloud to himself. He would reason with appearances. 'I see you, old Horny,' he said to the dead tree. And once, as dusk pursued him homeward, he began repeating:

As one that on a lonesome road
Doth walk in fear and dread,
And having once turned round, walks on,
And turns no more his head;
Because he knows a frightful fiend
Doth close behind him tread:

when the sound of a crackling twig made every nerve in his body stiffen with terror. Some impulse not his own snatched him round in the path, only to see old Luxmoor going out with his snares. Old Luxmoor touched his cap and grinned in an embarrassed way. Everyone knew that Luxmoor poached, but it was not polite to catch him at it. He did not appear to have overheard Titus or noticed his start of terror. But there had been one instant before recognition when Titus had almost known what he dreaded to see.

So it was pleasant to find that the company of his aunt could exorcise these ghostly enmities. Clearly, there was nothing in it. To-morrow he would go for a long walk by himself.

Laura also went for a walk that afternoon. It was a hot day, so hot and still that it felt like a Sunday. She could not do better than follow the example of the savages in Robinson Crusoe: go up on to a hill-top and say O! No pious savage could have ejaculated O! more devoutly than she did; for the hill-top was scattered over with patches of that small honey-scented flower called Tailors' Needles, and in conjunction with the austere outlines of the landscape this perfume was exquisitely sweet and surprising. She found a little green pit and sat down in it, leaning her back against the short firm turf. Ensconced in her private warmth and stillness she had almost fallen asleep when a moving figure on the opposite hillside caught her attention. Laura's grey eyes were very keen-sighted, she soon recognised that long stride and swinging gait. The solitary walker was Titus.

There is an amusing sense of superiority in seeing and remaining unseen. Laura sat up in her form and watched Titus attentively. He looked very small, human, and scrabbly, traversing that imperturbable surface. With such a large slope to wander upon, it was faintly comic to see Titus keeping so neatly to the path; the effect was rather as if he were being taken for a walk upon a string.

Further on the path was lost in a tangle of brambles and rusty foxglove stems which marked the site of Folly Wood, a larch plantation cut down during the war. In her map the wood had still been green. She had looked for it on one of her early explorations, and not finding it had felt defrauded. Her eyes now dwelt on the bramble tangle with annoyance. It was untidy, and fretted the hillside like a handful of rough-cast thrown on to a smooth wall. She turned back her gaze to see how Titus was getting on. It struck her that he was behaving rather oddly. Though he kept to the path he was walking almost like a drunken man or an idiot, now hurrying his pace, now reforming it into a staid deliberation that was certainly not his natural gait. Quite abruptly he began to run. He ran faster and faster, his feet striving on the slippery turf. He reached the outskirts of Folly Wood, and Laura could gauge the roughness of the going from his leaps and stumbles. Midway through the wood he staggered and fell full-length.

'A rabbit-hole,' she said. 'Now I suppose he's sprained his ankle.'

But before any thought of compunction could mitigate the rather scornful bewilderment with which she had been a spectator of these antics, Titus was up again, and behaving more oddly than ever. No amount of sprained ankle could warrant those raving gestures with which he beat himself, and beat the air. He seemed to be fending off an invisible volley of fisticuffs, for now he ducked his head, now he leaped to one side, now he threatened, now he quailed before a fresh attack. At last he made off with shambling speed, reeling and gesticulating as though his whole body bellowed with pain and fear. He reached the summit of the hill; for a moment he was silhouetted against the sky-line in a final convulsion of distress; then he was gone.

Laura felt as if she were releasing her gaze from a telescope. Her glance strayed about the landscape. She frowned and looked inquiringly from side to side, not able to credit her eyes. Blandly unconscious, the opposite hillside confronted her with its familiar face. A religious silence filled the valley. As the untroubled air had received Titus's roarings and damnings (for it was obvious that he had both roared and damned) without concerning itself to transmit them to her hearing, so her vision had absorbed his violent pantomime without concerning itself to alarm her brain. She could not reason about what she had seen; she could scarcely stir herself to feel any curiosity, and still less any sympathy. Like a masque of bears and fantastic shapes, it had seemed framed only to surprise and delight.

But that, she knew, was not Satan's way. He was not in the habit of bestowing these gratuitous peep-shows upon his servants, he was above the human weakness of doing things for fun; and if he exhibited Titus dancing upon the hillside like a cat on hot bricks, she might be sure that it was all according to plan. It behoved her to be serious and attend, instead of accepting it all in this spirit of blank entertainment. Even as a matter of bare civility she ought to find out what had happened. Besides, Titus might require her ministrations. She got up, and began to walk back to the village.

Titus, she reflected, would almost certainly have gone home. Even if he did not run all the way he would by now have had time to settle down and get over the worst of his disturbance. A kind of decency forbade her to view too immediately the dismay of her victim. Titus unmenaced, Titus invading her quiet and straddling over her peace of mind, was a very different thing from Titus melting and squirming before the fire of her resentment.

Now that she was walking to his assistance she felt quite sorry for him My nephew who is plagued by the Devil was as much an object for affectionate aunt-like interest as my nephew who has an attack of measles. She did not take the present affliction more seriously than she had taken those of the past. With time, and a change of air, she was confident that he would make a complete recovery.

As for her own share in the matter, she felt no shame at all. It had pleased Satan to come to her aid. Considering carefully, she did not see who else would have done so. Custom, public opinion, law, church, and state – all would have shaken their massive heads against her plea, and sent her back to bondage.

She reached Great Mop about five o'clock. As she turned up Mrs. Leak's garden-path, Titus bounded from the porch.

'There you are!' he exclaimed. 'We have just come to have tea with you.'

She perceived that Titus was not alone. In the porch playing with the kitten was Pandora Williams, Pandora Williams whom Titus had invited to play the rebeck at the Flower Show. Before Laura could welcome her Titus was exclaiming again.

'Such an afternoon as I've had! Such adventures! First I fell into a wasps'-nest, and then I got engaged to Pandora.'

So that was it. It was wasps. Wasps were the invisible enemies that had beset and routed him on the hill-side. O Beelzebub, God of flies! But why was he now going to marry Pandora Williams?

'The wops-nest was in Folly Wood. I tripped up, and fell smack on top of it. My God, I thought I should die! They got into my ears, and down my neck, and up my trousers, they were everywhere, as thick as spikes in soda-water. I ran for my life,

I ran nearly all the way home, and most of them came with me, either inside or out. And when I rushed up the street calling in an exhausted voice for onions, there was Pandora!'

'I had been invited to tea,' said Pandora rather primly.

'Yes, and I'd forgotten it, and gone out for a walk. Pandora, if I'd had my deserts, you would have scorned me, and left me to perish. Pandora, I shall never forget your magnanimous way of behaving. That was what did it, really. One has to offer marriage to a young woman who has picked dead wasps out of one's armpit.'

Laura had never seen Titus so excited. His face was flushed, his voice was loud, the pupils of his eyes were extraordinarily dilated. But how much of this was due to love and how much to wasps and witchcraft it was impossible to say. And was Pandora part of the witchcraft too, a sort of queen wasp whose sting was mortal balm I Why should Titus offer her marriage? Why should Pandora accept it? They had always been such friends.

Laura turned to the girl to see how she was taking it. Pandora's smooth cheeks and smooth lappets of black hair seemed to shed calm like an unwavering beam of moonlight. But at Laura's good wishes she started, and began nervously to counter them with explanations and apologies for coming to Laura's rooms for tea. She had dropped Titus' teapot, and broken it. Laura was not surprised that she had dropped the teapot. It was clear to her that Pandora's emotions that afternoon had been much more vehement than anything that Titus had experienced in his mental uproar. How well – thought Laura – she has hidden her feelings all this time! How well she is hiding them now!

These fine natures, she knew, always found comfort in cutting bread-and-butter. Pandora welcomed the suggestion. She covered three large plates, and would have covered a fourth if the butter had not given out. There were some ginger-bread nuts as well, and a few bull's-eyes. Mrs. Leak must have surmised a romance. She marked her sense of the occasion by the tea, which was almost purple – as strong as wedding-cake, Titus said.

It was a savagely plain tea. But had it consisted of cocoa and ship's-biscuit, Laura might have offered it without a qualm to guests so much absorbed by their proper emotions. Titus talked incessantly, and Pandora ate with the stealthy persistence of a bitch that gives suck. Meanwhile Laura looked at the new Mr. and Mrs. Willowes. They would do very well, she decided. Young as she was, Pandora had already the air of a family portrait; such looks, such characters change little, for they are independent of time. And undoubtedly she was very much in love with Titus. While he talked she watched his face with the utmost attention, though she did not seem to hear what he was saying. Titus, too, must be considerably in love. Despite the unreality of his behaviour, and a swelled nose, his happiness gave him an almost romantic appearance. Perhaps it was that too recently she had seen him dancing on the Devil's strings to be able to take him quite seriously; perhaps she was old-maidishly scornful of the authenticity of anything that a man may say or do; but at the back of her mind Laura felt that Titus was but a proxy wooer, the ambassador of an imperious dynastic will; and that the real match was made between Pandora and Lady Place.

Anyhow, it was all very suitable, and she must be content to leave it at that. The car from the Lamb and Flag was waiting to take them to the station. Titus was going back to London with Pandora to see her people, as Pandora had refused to face their approval alone. The Williamses lived pleasantly on Campden Hill, and were typical of the best class of Londoners, being almost indistinguishable from people living pleasantly in the country. What, indeed, could be more countrified than to be in town during September? For a moment Laura feared that she too would be obliged to travel to London. The lovers had insisted upon her company as far as the station.

'You must come,' said Titus. 'There will be all sorts of things I shall remember to ask you to do for me. I can't remember them now, but I shall the moment the car starts. I always do.'

Laura knew this to be very truth. Nevertheless she stood out against going until Pandora manoeuvred her into a corner and said in a desperate whisper: 'O Miss Willowes, for God's sake, please come. You've no idea how awful it is being left alone with someone you love.'

Laura replied: 'Very well. I'll come as a thank-offering.'

Pandora's sense of humour could just contrive a rather castaway smile.

They got into the car. There was no time to spare, and the driver took them along the winding lanes at top speed, sounding his horn incessantly. It was a closed car, and they sat in it in perfect silence all the way to the station. Before the car had drawn up in the station yard Titus leaped out and began to pay the driver. Then he looked wildly round for the train. There was no train in sight. It had not come in yet.

When Laura had seen them off and gone back to the station yard she found that in his excitement Titus had dismissed the driver without considering how his aunt was to get back to

Great Mop. However, it didn't matter – the bus started for Barleighs at half-past eight, and from Barleighs she could walk on for the rest of the way. This gave her an hour and a half to spend in Wickendon. A sensible way of passing the time would be to eat something before her return journey; but she was not hungry, and the fly-blown cafes in the High Street were not tempting. She bought some fruit, and turned up an alley between garden walls in search of a field where she could sit and eat it in peace. The alley soon changed to an untidy lane and then to a cinder-track running steeply uphill between high hedges. A municipal kindliness had supplied at intervals iron benches, clamped and riveted into the cinders. But no one reposed on them, and the place was unpeopled save by swarms of midges. Laura was hot and breathless by the time she reached the top of the hill and came out upon a bare grassy common. Here was an obvious place to sit down and gasp, and as there were no iron benches to deter her, she did so. But she immediately forgot her exhaustion, so arresting was the site that lay before her.

The cinder-track led to a small enclosure, full of cypresses, yews, clipped junipers and weepingwillows. Rising from this funereal plumage was an assortment of minarets, gilded cupolas and obelisks. She stared at this phenomenon, so byronic in conception, so spick and span in execution, and sprouting so surprisingly from the mild Chiltern landscape, completely at a loss to account for it. Then she remembered: it was the Maulgrave Folly. She had read of it in the guide-book, and of its author, Sir Ralph Maulgrave, the Satanic Baronet, the libertine, the atheist, who drank out of a skull, who played away his mistress and pistolled the winner, who rode about Buckinghamshire on a zebra, whose conversation had been too much for

Thomas Moore. 'This bad and eccentric character,' the guide-book said, disinfecting his memory with rational amusement. Grown old, he had amused himself by elaborating a burial-place which was to be an epitome of his eclectic and pessimistic opinions. He must, thought Laura, have spent many hours on this hillside, watching the masons and directing the gardeners where to plant his cypresses. And afterwards he would be wheeled away in his bath-chair, for, pace the guide-book, at a comparatively early age he lost the use of his legs.

Poor gentleman, how completely he had misunderstood the Devil! The plethoric gilt cupolas winked in the setting sun. For all their bad taste, they were perfectly respectable – cupolas and minarets and cypresses, all had a sleek and well-cared-for look. They had an assured income, nothing could disturb their calm. The silly, vain, passionate heart that lay buried there had bequeathed a sum of money for their perpetual upkeep. The Satanic Baronet who mocked at eternal life and designed this place as a lasting testimony of his disbelief had contrived to immortalise himself as a laughing-stock.

It was ungenerous. The dead man had been pilloried long enough; it was high time that Maulgrave's Folly should be left to fall into decent ruin and decay. And instead of that, even at this moment it was being trimmed up afresh. She felt a thrill of anger as she saw a gardener come out of the enclosure, carrying a flag basket and a pair of shears. He came towards her, and something about the rather slouching and prowling gait struck her as being familiar. She looked more closely, and recognised Satan.

'How can you?' she said, when he was within speaking distance. He, of all people, should be more compassionate to the shade of Sir Ralph.

He feigned not to hear her.

'Would you care to go over the Folly, ma'am?' he inquired. 'It's quite a curiosity. Visitors come out from London to see it.'

Laura was not going to be fubbed off like this. He might pretend not to recognise her, but she would jog his memory.

'So you are a grave-keeper as well as a gamekeeper?'

'The Council employ me to cut the bushes,' he answered.

'O Satan!' she exclaimed, hurt by his equivocations. 'Do you always hide?'

With the gesture of a man who can never hold out against women, he yielded and sat down beside her on the grass.

Laura felt a momentary embarrassment. She had long wished for a reasonable conversation with her Master, but now that her wish seemed about to be granted, she felt rather at a loss for an opening. At last she observed:

'Titus has gone.'

'Indeed? Isn't that rather sudden? It was only this afternoon that I met him.'

'Yes, I saw you meeting him. At least, I saw him meeting you.'

'Just so. It is remarkable,' he added, as though he were politely parrying her thought, 'how invisible one is on these bare green hillsides.'

'Or in these thick brown woods,' said Laura, rather sternly.

This sort of Satanic playfulness was no novelty; Vinegar often behaved in the same fashion, leaping about just out of reach when she wanted to catch him and shut him up indoors.

'Or in these thick brown woods,' he concurred. 'Folly Wood is especially dense.'

'Is?'

'Is. Once a wood, always a wood.'

Once a wood, always a wood. The words rang true, and she sat silent, considering them. Pious Asa might hew down the groves, but as far as the Devil was concerned he hewed in vain. Once a wood, always a wood: trees where he sat would crowd into a shade. And people going by in broad sunlight would be aware of slow voices overhead, and a sudden chill would fall upon their flesh. Then, if like her. they had a natural leaning towards the Devil, they would linger, listening about them with half-dosed eyes and averted senses; but if they were respectable people like Henry and Caroline they would talk rather louder and hurry on. There remaineth a rest for the people of God (somehow the thought of the Devil always propelled her mind to the Holy Scriptures), and for the other people, the people of Satan, there remained a rest also. Held fast in that strong memory no wild thing could be shaken, no secret covert destroyed, no haunt of shadow and silence laid open. The goods yard at Paddington, for instance – a savage place! as holy and enchanted as ever it had been. Not one of the monuments and tinkerings of man could impose on the Satanic mind. The Vatican and the Crystal Palace, and all the neat human nest-boxes in rows, Balham and Fulham and the Cromwell Road – he saw through them, they went flop like cardhouses, the bricks were earth again, and the steel girders burrowed shrieking into the veins of earth, and the dead timber was restored to the ghostly groves. Wolves howled through the streets of Paris, the foxes played in the throneroom of Schonbrunn, and in the basement at Apsley Terrace the mammoth slowly revolved, trampling out its lair.

'Then I needn't really have come here to meet you!' she exclaimed.

'Did you?'

'I didn't know I did. I thought I came here to be in the country, and to escape being an aunt.'

'Titus came here to write a book on Fuseli, and to enjoy himself.'

'Titus! I can't believe you wanted him?

'But you do believe I wanted you.'

Rather taken aback she yet answered the Devil honestly.

'Yes! I do believe you wanted me. Though really I don't know why you should.'

A slightly malevolent smile crossed the Devil's face. For some reason or other her modesty seemed to have netted him.

'Some people would say that you had flung yourself at my head.'

'Other people,' she retorted, 'would say that you had been going about seeking to devour me.'

'Exactly. I even roared that night. But you were asleep while I roared. Only the hills heard me triumphing over my spoil.'

Laura said: 'I wish I could really believe that.'

'I wish you could, too,' he answered affably; 'you would feel so comfortable and important. But you won't, although it is much more probable than you might suppose.'

Laura stretched herself out on the turf and pillowed her head on her arm.

'Nothing could feel more comfortable than I do, now that Titus is gone,' she said. 'And as for importance, I never wish to feel important again. I had enough of that when I was an aunt.'

'Well, you're a witch now.'

'Yes.... I really am, aren't I?'

'Irrevocably.'

His voice was so perfectly grave that she began to suspect him of concealing some amusement When but a moment before he had jested she had thought a deeper meaning lay beneath his words, she almost believed that his voice had roared over her in the thunder. If he had spoken without feigning then, she had not heard him; for he had stopped her ears with a sleep.

'Why do you sigh?' he asked.

'Did I sigh? I'm puzzled, that's all. You see, although I'm a witch, and although you sitting here beside me tell me so, I can't really appreciate it, take it in. It all seems perfectly natural.'

'That is because you are in my power. No servant of mine can feel remorse, or doubt, or surprise. You may be quite easy, Laura: you will never escape me, for you can never wish to.'

'Yes, I can quite well believe that, I'm sure I shall never wish to escape you. But you are a mysterious Master.'

'You seem to me rather an exacting servant. I have shaped myself like a jobbing gardener, I am sitting on the grass beside you (I'll have one of your apples if I may. They are a fruit I am particularly fond of), I am doing everything in my power to be agreeable and reassuring... What more do you want?'

'That is exactly what I complain of. You are too lifelike to be natural; why, it might be Goethe's Conversations with Eckermann. No! if I am really a witch, treat me as such. Satisfy my curiosity. Tell me about yourself.'

'Tell me first what you think,' he answered.

'I think' – she began cautiously (while he hid his cards it would not do to show all hers) – 'I think you are a kind of black knight, wandering about and succouring decayed gentlewomen.'

'There are warlocks too, remember.'

'I can't take warlocks so seriously, not as a class. It is we witches who count. We have more need of you. Women have such vivid imaginations, and lead such dull lives. Their pleasure in life is so soon over; they are so dependent upon others, and their dependence so soon becomes a nuisance. Do you understand?'

He was silent. She continued, slowly, knitting her brows in the effort to make clear to herself and him the thought that was in her mind:

'It's like this. When I think of witches, I seem to see all over England, all over Europe, women living and growing old, as common as blackberries, and as unregarded. I see them, wives and sisters of respectable men, chapel members, and blacksmiths, and small farmers, and Puritans. In places like Bedfordshire, the sort of country one sees from the train. You know. Well, there they were, there they are, child-rearing, house-keeping, hanging washed dishcloths on currant bushes; and for diversion each other's silly conversation, and listening to men talking together in the way that men talk and women listen. Quite different to the way women talk, and men listen, if they listen at all. And all the time being thrust further down into dullness when the one thing all women hate is to be thought dull. And on Sundays they put on plain stuff gowns and starched white coverings on their heads and necks – the Puritan ones did – and walked across the fields to chapel, and listened to the sermon. Sin and Grace, and God and the—' (she stopped herself just in time), 'and St. Paul. All men's things, like politics, or mathematics. Nothing for them except subjection and plaiting their hair. And on the way back they listened to more talk. Talk about the sermon, or war, or cock-fighting; and when they got back, there were the potatoes to be cooked for dinner. It sounds very petty to complain about, but I tell you, that sort of thing settles down on one like a fine dust, and by and by the dust is age, settling down. Settling down! You never die, do you? No doubt that's far worse, but there is a dreadful kind of dreary immortality about being settled down on by one day after another. And they think how they were young once, and they see new young women, just like what they were, and yet as surprising as if it had never happened before, like trees in spring. But they are like trees towards the end of summer, heavy and dusty, and nobody finds their leaves surprising, or notices them till they fall off. If they could be passive and unnoticed, it wouldn't matter. But they must be active, and still not noticed. Doing, doing, doing, till mere habit scolds at them like a housewife, and rouses them up – when they might sit in their doorways and think – to be doing still!' She paused, out of breath. She had never made such a long speech in the whole of her life, nor spoken with such passion. She scarcely knew what she had said, and felt giddy and unaccustomed, as though she had been thrown into the air and had suddenly begun to fly.

The Devil was silent, and looked thoughtfully at the ground. He seemed to be rather touched by all this. She continued, for she feared that if she did not go on talking she would grow ashamed at having said so much.

'Is it true that you can poke the fire with a stick of dynamite in perfect safety? I used to take my nieces to scientific lectures, and I believe I heard it then. Anyhow, even if it isn't true of dynamite, it's true of women. But they know they are dynamite, and long for the concussion that may justify them. Some may get religion, then they're all right, I expect. But for the others, for so many, what can there be but witchcraft? That strikes them real. Even if other people still find them quite safe and usual, and go on poking with them, they know in their hearts how dangerous, how incalculable, how extraordinary they are. Even if they never do anything with their witchcraft, they know it's there – ready! Respectable countrywomen keep their grave-clothes in a corner of the chest of drawers, hidden away, and when they want a little comfort they go and look at them, and think that once more, at any rate, they will be worth dressing with care. But the witch keeps her cloak of darkness, her dress embroidered with signs and planets; that's better worth looking at. And think, Satan, what a compliment you pay her, pursuing her soul, lying in wait for it, following it through all its windings, crafty and patient and secret like a gentleman out killing tigers. Her soul – when no one else would give a look at her body even! And they are all so accustomed, so sure of her! They say: "Dear Lolly! What shall we give her for her birthday this year? Perhaps a hot-water bottle. Or what about a nice black lace scarf? Or a new workbox f Her old one is nearly worn out." But you say: "Come here, my bird! I will give you the dangerous black night to stretch your wings in, and poisonous berries to feed on, and a nest made of bones and thorns, perched high up in danger where no one can climb to it." That's why we become witches: to show our scorn of pretending life's a safe business, to satisfy our passion for adventure. It's not malice, or wickedness – well, perhaps it is wickedness, for most women love that – but certainly not malice, not wanting to plague cattle and make horrid children spout up pins and – what is it?—"blight the genial bed." Of course, given the power, one may go in for that sort of thing, either in self-defence, or just out of playfulness. But it's a poor twopenny housewifely kind of witchcraft, black magic is, and white magic is no better. One doesn't become a witch to run round being harmful, or to run round being helpful either, a district visitor on a broomstick. It's to escape all that – to have a life of one's own, not an existence doled out to you by others, charitable refuse of their thoughts, so many ounces of stale bread of life a day, the workhouse dietary is scientifically calculated to support life. As for the witches who can only express themselves by pins and bed-blighting, they have been warped into that shape by the dismal lives they've led. Think of Miss Carloe! She's a typical witch, people would say. Really she's the typical genteel spinster who's spent herself being useful to people who didn't want her. If you'd got her younger she'd never be like that.'

'You seem to know a good deal about witches,' remarked Satan. 'But you were going to say what you thought about me.'

She shook her head.

'Go on,' he said encouragingly. 'You have compared me to a knight-errant. That's very pretty. I believe you have also compared me to a hunter, a poaching sort of hunter, prowling through the woods after dark. Not so flattering to my vanity as the knight-errant, but more accurate, I daresay.'

'O Satan! Why do you encourage me to talk when you know all my thoughts?'

'I encourage you to talk, not that I may know all your thoughts, but that you may. Go on, Laura. Don't be foolish. What do you think about me?'

'I don't know,' she said honestly. 'I don't think I do think. I only rhapsodise and make comparisons. You're beyond me, my thought flies off you like the centrifugal hypothesis. And after this I shall be more at a loss than ever, for I like you so much, I find you so kind and sympathetic. But it is obvious that you can't be merely a benevolent institution. No, I must be your witch in blindness.'

'You don't take warlocks so seriously, I know. But you might find their point of view illuminating. As it's a spiritual difficulty, why not consult Mr. Jones?'

'Poor Mr. Jones!' Laura began to laugh. 'He can't call his soul his own.'

'Hush! Have you forgotten that he has sold it to me?'

'Then why did you mortgage it to Mr. Gurdon? Mr. Jones isn't even allowed to attend the Sabbath.'

'You are a little dense at times. Hasn't it occurred to you that other people might share your sophisticated dislike for the Sabbath?'

'You don't attend the Sabbath either, if it comes to that.'

'How do you know? Don't try to put me in your pocket, Laura. You are not my only conquest, and I am not a human master to have favourites among my servants. All are souls that come to my net. I apologise for the pun, but it is apt.'

She had been rebuked, but she did not feel particularly abashed. It was true, then, what she had read of the happy relationship between the Devil and his servants. If Euphan Macalzean had rated him – why, so, at a pinch, might she. Other things that she had read might also be true, she thought, things that she had till now been inclined to reject. So easygoing a Master who had no favourites among his servants might in reality attend the Sabbath, might unbend enough to eat black-puddings at a picnic without losing his dignity.

'That offensive young man at the Sabbath,' she remarked, 'I know he wasn't you. Who was he?'

'He's one of these brilliant young authors,' replied the Devil. 'I believe Titus knows him. He sold me his soul on the condition that once a week he should be without doubt the most important person at a party.'

'Why didn't he sell his soul in order to become a great writer? Then he could have had the party into the bargain.'

'He preferred to take a short-cut, you see.'

She didn't see. But she was too proud to inquire further, especially as Satan was now smiling at her as if she were a pet lamb.

'What did Mr. Jones—'

'That's enough! You can ask him that yourself, when you take your lessons in demonology.'

'Do you suppose for one moment that Mr. Gurdon would let me sit closeted with Mr. Jones taking lessons in plain needlework even? He would put his face in at the window and say: "How much longer are them Mothers to be kept waiting?" or: "I should like to know what your reverence is doing about that there dung?" or: "I suppose you know that the cowman's girl may go off at any minute." And then he'd take him down to the shrubbery and scold him. My heart bleeds for the poor old gentleman!'

'Mr. Jones' – Satan spoke demurely – 'will have his reward in another life.'

Laura was silent. She gazed at the Maulgrave Folly with what she could feel to be a pensive expression. But her mind was a blank.

'A delicate point, you say? Perhaps it is bad taste on my part to jest about it.'

A midge settled on Laura's wrist. She smacked at it.

'Dead!' said Satan.

The word dropped into her mind like a pebble thrown into a pond. She had heard it so often, and now she heard it once more. The same waves of thought circled outwards, waves of startled thought spreading out on all sides, rocking the shadows of familiar things, blurring the steadfast pictures of trees and clouds, circling outward one after the other, each wave more listless, more imperceptible than the last, until the pool was still again.

There might be some questions that even the Devil could not answer. She turned her eyes to him with their question.

Satan had risen to his feet. He picked up the flag basket and the shears, and made ready to go.

'Is it time?' asked Laura.

He nodded, and smiled.

She got up in her turn, and began to shake the dust off her skirt. Then she prodded a hole for the bag which had held the apples, and buried it tidily, smoothing the earth over the hole. This took a little time to do, and when she looked round for Satan, to say good-bye, he was out of sight.

Seeing that he was gone she sat down again, for she wanted to think him over. A pleasant conversation, though she had done most of the talking. The tract of flattened grass at her side showed where he had rested, and there was the rampion flower he had held in his hand. Grass that has been lain upon has always a rather popular bank-holidayish look, and even the Devil's lair was not exempt from this. It was as though the grass were in league with him, faithfully playing-up to his pose of being a quite everyday phenomenon. Not a blade of grass was signed, not a clover-leaf blasted, and the rampion flower was withering quite naturally; yet he who had sat there was Satan, the author of all evil, whose thoughts were a darkness, whose roots went down into the pit. There was no action too mean for him, no instrument too petty; he would go into a milk-jug to work mischief. And presently he would emerge, imperturbable, inscrutable, enormous with the dignity of natural behaviour and untrammelled self-fulfilment.

To be this – a character truly integral, a perpetual flowering of power and cunning from an undivided will – was enough to constitute the charm and majesty of the Devil. No cloak of terrors was necessary to enlarge that stature, and to suppose him capable of speculation or metaphysic would be like offering to crown him with a few casual straws. Very probably he was quite stupid. When she had asked him about death he had got up and gone away, which looked as if he did not know much more about it than she did herself: indeed, being immortal, it was unlikely that he would know as much. Instead, his mind brooded immovably over the landscape and over the natures of men, an unforgetting and unchoosing mind. That, of course – and she jumped up in her excitement and began to wave her arms – was why he was the Devil, the enemy of souls. His memory was too long, too retentive; there was no appeasing its witness, no hoodwinking it with the present; and that was why at one stage of civilisation people said he was the embodiment of all evil, and then a little later on that he didn't exist.

For a moment Laura thought that she had him: and on the next, as though he had tricked himself out of her grasp, her thoughts were scattered by the sudden consciousness of a sort of jerk in the atmosphere. The sun had gone down, sliding abruptly behind the hills. In that case the bus would have gone too, she might as well hope to catch the one as the other. First Satan, then the sun and the bus – adieu, mes gens! With affectionate unconcern she seemed to be waving them farewell, pleased to be left to herself, left to enter into this new independence acknowledged by their departure.

The night was at her disposal. She might walk back to Great Mop and arrive very late: or she might sleep out and not trouble to arrive till to-morrow. Whichever she did Mrs. Leak would not mind. That was one of the advantages of dealing with witches; they do not mind if you are a little odd in your ways, frown if you are late for meals, fret if you are out all night, pry and commiserate when at length you return. Lovely to be with people who prefer their thoughts to yours, lovely to live at your own sweet will, lovely to sleep out all night! She had quite decided, now, to do so. It was an adventure, she had never done such a thing before, and yet it seemed most natural. She would not sleep here: Wickendon was too close. But presently, later on, when she felt inclined to, she would wander off in search of a suitable dry ditch or an accommodatingly loosened haystack; or wading through last year's leaves and this year's fern she would penetrate into a wood and burrow herself a bed. Satan going his rounds might come upon her and smile to see her lying so peaceful and secure in his dangerous keeping. But he would not disturb her. Why should he? The pursuit was over, as far as she was concerned. She could sleep where she pleased, a hind couched in the Devil's coverts, a witch made free of her

Master's immunity; while he, wakeful and stealthy, was already out after new game. So he would not disturb her. A closer darkness upon her slumber, a deeper voice in the murmuring leaves overhead – that would be all she would know of his undesiring and unjudging gaze, his satisfied but profoundly indifferent ownership.

PAPERBACK FICTION

- 21 Short Tales by Franz Kafka, ISBN: 9789354991103
- A Christmas Carol by Charles Dickens, ISBN: 9788193545874
- A Little Princess by Frances Hodgson Burnett, ISBN: 9789354990861
- A Midsummer Night's Dream by William Shakespeare, ISBN: 9789380914510
- A Modest Proposal and Other Stories by Jonathan Swift, ISBN: 9789354994609
- A Portrait of Artist as a Young Man by James Joyce, ISBN: 9789354994623
- A Room of One's Own by Virginia Woolf, ISBN: 9789354990281
- A Room with A View by E. M. Forster, ISBN: 9789354994630
- A Streetcar Named Desire by Tennessee Williams, ISBN: 9788194748601
- A Tear and a Smile by Kahlil Gibran, ISBN: 9788180320477
- Alice's Adventures in Wonderland by Lewis Carroll, ISBN: 9789380914046
- Arms and the Man by George Bernard Shaw, ISBN: 9789354994159
- Around the World in Eighty Days by Jules Verne, ISBN: 9789354994647
- As I Lay Dying by William Faulkner, ISBN: 9789390492381
- As You Like It by William Shakespeare, ISBN: 9789380914459
- Black Beauty by Anna Sewell, ISBN: 9788180320095
- Burmese Days by George Orwell, ISBN: 9789354991110
- Dracula by Bram Stoker, ISBN: 9789354994708
- Fav. Tales from the Arabian Nights by Richard F. Burton, ISBN: 9789380914077
- First Love by Ivan Turgenev, ISBN: 9789354994715
- Frankenstein by Mary Shelley, ISBN: 9789354994784
- Gitanjali by Rabindranath Tagore, ISBN: 9789380914886
- Gone with the Wind by Margaret Mitchell, ISBN: 9789390492787
- Great American Short Stories by Various Authors, ISBN: 9789380914060
- Great German Short Stories by Various Authors, ISBN: 9789380914053

Develop your reading habit | **Gift books to your friends**

PAPERBACK FICTION

- Great Horror Stories by Various Authors, ISBN: 9789380914084
- Heidi by Johanna Spyri, ISBN: 9789354994166
- In Our Time and Other Stories by Ernest Hemingway, ISBN: 9789354994791
- Joy in the Morning by P.G. Wodehouse, ISBN: 9789354994449
- Julius Caesar by William Shakespeare, ISBN: 9789380914374
- Macbeth by William Shakespeare, ISBN: 9789380914343
- Man and Superman by George Bernard Shaw, ISBN: 9789354994470
- Metamorphosis by Franz Kafka, ISBN: 9788180320057
- Mother by Maxim Gorky, ISBN: 9788180320330
- One, None and a Hundred Thousand by Luigi Pirandello, ISBN: 9789389716337
- Othello by William Shakespeare, ISBN: 9789380914404
- Pride and Prejudice by Jane Austen, ISBN: 9789380914428
- Romeo and Juliet by William Shakespeare, ISBN: 9789380914329
- Selected Short Stories of James Joyce by James Joyce, ISBN: 9788180320392
- Selected Short Stories of Friedrich Nietzsche, ISBN: 9788180320491
- Selected Stories of Rabindranath Tagore, ISBN: 9789380914770
- Sense and Sensibility by Jane Austen, ISBN: 9789380914589
- Tales from India by Rudyard Kipling, ISBN: 9789380914411
- Tales from Shakespeare by Charles & Mary Lamb, ISBN: 9789380914367
- The Autobiography of Benjamin Franklin, ISBN: 9788190276689
- The Beautiful and Damned by F. Scott Fitzgerald, ISBN: 9789354994548
- The Blue Castle by Lucy Maud Montgomery, ISBN: 9789354994227
- The Canterville Ghost by Oscar Wilde, ISBN: 9789380914527
- The Great Gatsby by F. Scott Fitzgerald, ISBN: 9789380914473
- The Hound of the Baskervilles by Sir Arthur Conan Doyle, ISBN: 9789380914534

Develop your reading habit | **Gift books to your friends**

PAPERBACK FICTION

- The House Without a Key by Earl Derr Biggers, ISBN: 9789354991561
- The Invisible Man by H.G. Wells, ISBN: 9788193545850
- The Journey to the East by Hermann Hesse, ISBN: 9789354994241
- The Jungle by Upton Sinclair, ISBN: 9789354994555
- The Man in the Brown Suit by Agatha Christie, ISBN: 9789390492497
- The Man Who Was Thursday by Gilbert K. Chesterton, ISBN: 9789354990939
- The Painted Veil by W. Somerset Maugham, ISBN: 9789354990946
- The Pilgrim's Progress by John Bunyan, ISBN: 9789354991776
- The Prince by Niccolò Machiavelli, ISBN: 9789387669024
- The Red Badge of Courage by Stephen Crane, ISBN: 9789354990977
- The Secret Adversary by Agatha Christie, ISBN: 9789390492565
- The Sound and the Fury by William Faulkner, ISBN: 9789390492572
- The Time Machine by HG Wells, ISBN: 9789387669048
- The Trial by Franz Kafka, ISBN: 9789390492596
- The War of the Worlds by H.G. Wells, ISBN: 9789354991936
- The Wind in the Willows by Kenneth Grahame, ISBN: 9789354992018
- The Yellow Wallpaper and Other Stories by C.P. Gilman, ISBN: 9789354992056
- Three Men in a Boat by Jerome K. Jerome, ISBN: 9789380914442
- To the Lighthouse by Virginia Woolf, ISBN: 9789390492190
- Treasure Island by Robert Louis Stevenson, ISBN: 9788193545881
- We by Yevgeny Zamyatin, ISBN: 9789354992087
- White Fang by Jack London, ISBN: 9789354994616
- World's Best Short Stories: Volume 1 by Various Authors, ISBN: 9789390492275
- World's Best Short Stories: Volume 2 by Various Authors, ISBN: 9789354992278
- Wuthering Heights by Emily Brontë, ISBN: 9788193545898

Develop your reading habit | **Gift books to your friends**